Myths are universal and timeless stories that reflect and shape our lives — they explore our desires, our fears, our longings and provide narratives that remind us what it means to be human. *The Myths* series brings together some of the world's finest writers, each of whom has retold a myth in a contemporary and memorable way. Authors in the series include: Chinua Achebe, Karen Armstrong, Margaret Atwood, AS Byatt, Michel Faber, David Grossman, Milton Hatoum, Natsuo Kirino, Alexander McCall Smith, Tomás Eloy Martínez, Klas Östergren, Victor Pelevin, Ali Smith, Donna Tartt, Su Tong, Dubravka Ugresic, Salley Vickers and Jeanette Winterson.

BINU AND
THE GREAT WALL

Su Tong

Translated from the Chinese by
Howard Goldblatt

ISIS

LARGE PRINT

Oxford

First published in Great Britain 2007
by
Canongate Books Ltd.

Published in Large Print 2008 by ISIS Publishing Ltd.,
7 Centremead, Osney Mead, Oxford OX2 0ES
by arrangement with
Canongate Books Ltd.

British Library Cataloguing in Publication Data
Tong, Su 1963–
      Binu and the Great Wall. – Large print ed.
      1. Quests (Expeditions) – Fiction
      2. Great Wall of China (China) – Fiction
      3. China – History – Qin dynasty,
      221–207 B. C. – Fiction
      4. Legends
      5. Large type books
      I. Title
      895.1'352 [F]

            ISBN 978–0–7531–8062–4 (hb)
            ISBN 978–0–7531–8063–1 (pb)

Printed and bound in Great Britain by
T. J. International Ltd., Padstow, Cornwall

Preface

The tale of Binu wailing at the Great Wall has been passed down through generations for two millennia in China; a story that has been told again and again by ordinary people. Mine is only the latest retelling, but blessed with the added good fortune of finding its way beyond China's borders.

In one sense, myths are soaring realities; when troubling realities soar, they may remain troubling, but they afford the people experiencing those realities the opportunity to escape for a short time: a welcome escape, and a necessary one.

The most beautiful, uninhibited imagination invariably comes from ordinary people. To a large extent, I wrote this book to re-imagine the emotional lives of these people, the distillation of which, in my view, forms a sort of popular philosophy. In effect the writing process became an inquiry into this particular imagined realm.

The wild imaginings of all humanity are structured by people's emotional landscapes; fundamental principles of freedom, equality, and justice co-exist both in our real and imagined lives. Myths instil in us a special way of thinking; what exists in the quotidian world but can also make the leap to paradigms that surpass life bestows on us an extraordinary reason to live. Where myths are created, the world offers a succinct but warm contour: life and death, entrances and exits are given natural, if emblematic, reasonings; cruel, harsh, real-life problems can be resolved.

In the mythical tale of Binu (or as she is known more formally, Meng Jiangnü), a woman's tears bring the Great Wall crashing down; it is an optimistic tale, not a sorrowful one. Rather than characterize it as a woman's tears bringing an end to the drawn-out search for her husband, we might say that those tears enable her to resolve one of life's great predicaments.

How one relates a tale that everyone already knows is a problem that all writers face. There is a Binu in the heart of everyone; my understanding of her comprises an exploration of gender, the recognition of a pure heart, the recollection of a long absent emotion; my understanding of her fate is a realisation of suffering and existence. Binu's story is a legend not so much about a woman at the bottom of society, but rather a legend about status and social class.

I have seen the Great Wall, and I have visited the Meng Jiangnü Temple. But I have never seen Binu. Who has? She is set adrift in narrative history and takes on many forms. I have attempted to give her a rope, one that can stretch across two thousand years, allowing her to pull me along with her; like Binu, I want to go to the Great Wall.

CONTENTS

Crying

The people who live at the foot of North Mountain cannot cry, even today. Grey-haired adults seize the opportunity to instruct future generations; they point to North Mountain and recall the tragedy that occurred so many years ago.

"Child," they say, "other people's ancestors lie beneath the ground, but the spirits of our ancestors roam the slopes of North Mountain. Why do you think those white butterflies flit about the mountain? And what about the scarab beetles that scurry back and forth across mountain paths? They are the spirits of our ancestors who were wronged; that is why. They are trying to find their North Mountain gravesites. Other people's ancestors died of starvation and illness, or of old age, or in war. But our ancestors died of injustice. Guess, child, I want you to guess. Why did they die? Ah, you can guess all you want, but you will never get the right answer. Their eyes were the cause of their deaths; they drowned in their own tears!"

The wild vegetation on the mountain was ideal for eating and its spring water perfect for drinking — except for the water in the pool that formed when water ran down the mountain slope and into Lord Xintao's empty grave — according to the Kindling Village sorceresses, who were the source of all local knowledge. No one now could recall what Lord Xintao had looked like when he lived as a hermit on North Mountain, but no one dared drink that water, for that would be tantamount to drinking from a pool of tears, the accumulated tears of three hundred ancient spirits, covered by a layer of sweet rainwater.

Lord Xintao's funeral had alarmed the king; he forbade people to cry and positioned armies of court officials and prefecture soldiers half-way up the mountain to examine mourners as they came down the mountain. Some passed through the blockade without incident, others were stopped, their cheeks and eyes subjected to intense scrutiny; three hundred villagers whose tears had yet to dry were detained half-way down the mountain. The tears they had shed at Lord Xintao's funeral were about to cost them their lives.

High officials and members of the royalty knew of the new law, but not the villagers who lived at the foot of North Mountain. Blue Cloud Prefecture and the cities of the north were far off on the other side of the mountain; news of the outside world seldom reached them. All year round, they talked only of tilling fields and planting crops. Long after it had happened, the people learned that Lord Xintao had been exiled to North Mountain by the King, his back tattooed in gold with the King's command, condemning him to death in a frozen climate. But Lord Xintao lived on until Qingming, the day set aside for sweeping graves, when he looped a strip of white silk over a beam in his hut and hanged himself. The people living at the foot of the mountain, simple folk who held stubbornly to their beliefs, knew only that Lord Xintao was the King's uncle; his royal blood alone made him deserving of their reverence, and added to that was respect for anyone who lived the life of a recluse. On the day of his funeral they ran down the mountain, overcome with sorrow for the departed and unaware that their tears were to be their undoing.

To this day, the villagers at the foot of North Mountain dare not shed a tear on pain of death.

The descendants of the weeping spirits were scattered throughout the Peach Village, Kindling Village and Millstone Village area, where even young children understood their ancestry. In Peach Village and Millstone Village, the right to cry was, in the main, determined by age. Once a child learned to walk, he was no longer permitted to cry. The residents of Kindling Village, on the other side of the river, imposed an outright prohibition on crying, with no exceptions, not even for newborn babies; the honour or disgrace of these "opposite-bank" residents was directly linked to their sons' and daughters' tear ducts. Village women, in an impassioned attempt to hold their heads up in the company of others, sought the ministrations of sorcerers, and most of the clever women had command of the proper magic to prevent crying: they fed their infants a concoction of mother's milk and juice of wolfberry and mulberry; when the recipients of this red liquid were fully fed, they fell into a long, peaceful sleep. There were occasional recalcitrant children whom no one seemed able to stop from crying, making the Kindling Village mothers worry endlessly. They had a secret means of relieving their vexations, so mysterious it invited all sorts of fantastic speculation. Residents of neighbouring villages would gaze across the river and wonder at the peace and quiet of Kindling Village, that and the visible decrease in its population. The primary cause of both, they concluded, was the absence of crying children. Those children who cried — how could they all simply disappear?

The impoverished state of North Mountain persisted, like the rapids of the nearby Millstone River. No one knew where the water flowed to, but every drop had its source, and so the people searched beneath the sky and above the ground, seeking the sources of their own sons and daughters. The heavens heralded the boys' arrival; soon after their sons were born, proud parents looked heavenward, where they saw the sun, the moon, the stars, soaring birds and floating clouds; whatever they saw was what their sons would be, which is why some of the boys at the foot of North Mountain were the sun and stars, some were eagles, others were rain, and the very least of them was a single cloud. But when girls came into this world, gloom settled over the huts and shacks, and to escape a blood curse the fathers were required to stride thirty-three paces from their front door. They headed east at a brisk pace, heads down, and whatever the ground revealed at the thirty-third pace was what their daughters would become. Naturally, they avoided pig sties and chicken coops, and

4

long-legged fathers could reach the wildwoods at the far edge of the village; even so, the sources of daughters were humble and base. Most would belong to wild greens, melons, fruits and the like: a mushroom, a lichen, a dry weed, a wild chrysanthemum, or perhaps a mollusc, a puddle, or a goose feather — and these were girls who enjoyed a relatively decent fate. The future for the remaining girls, those who would become cow patties, earthworms, or beetles, induced indescribable anxieties in parents.

Boys who came from the sky were, by definition, expansive and steadfast, and the prohibition on crying was easier for them to sustain. A good boy knew how to swallow his tears, a character trait in keeping with the principles of heaven and earth, and even with crying boys the problem was easily remedied: from their youngest days, they were told that those disgraceful tears could exit the body through their penises, and so, whenever a parent spotted signs in their children's eyes that tears were on their way, they would hurriedly push them out of the door and say, "Go and pee, hurry up and pee!" It was the girls who most readily violated the prohibition of crying, but this had been decided by fate. Grass poking out of the ground is saddened by the wind; sweet flag floating at the water's edge is drenched when it rains; and that is why stories about crying are always about girls.

People at the foot of North Mountain raised their sons differently but with similar results; when it came to raising girls, however, each village had its own *Rulebook for Daughters*. The one they followed in

Millstone Village was rather coarse and crude, and slightly passive: with an emphasis on strength, the girls there grew up playing with boys, for whom crying and peeing were inextricably linked; young women saw nothing shameful in lifting their skirts and squatting on the ground when the urge to cry came upon them, and as soon as there was a puddle on the ground beneath them, their sadness evaporated. Malicious outsiders liked to talk about Millstone Village girls who, even when they reached marrying age, still squatted in full view! They could wear their prettiest clothes, but the hems of their skirts always smelled bad!

The Kindling Village *Rulebook for Daughters* was full of sorcery, mysteries and darkness. In villages with a sorceress, chimney smoke rose straight into the sky day and night. The girls living there never cried and never smiled; they went down to the river to collect dead fish and the bones of dead animals, their every movement exactly the same as their mothers' before them, from childhood through to old age. Some Kindling Village girls exhibited a dull, weathered look; after long periods of using bovine bones and tortoise shells to probe the fates of others, they neglected their own, and when they mourned the death of a son or a husband they habitually smeared a mixture of crow droppings and oven ashes around their eyes so that, no matter how deep the sorrow, they were able to mask it. Precise formulas and mysterious magic sapped their energy and turned their faces gaunt and sallow. When people on the riverbank spotted a Kindling Village girl, they felt an indescribable depression. Why, they wondered, did those girls lack youthfulness? Girls in their early teens and older women with dishevelled hair and dirty faces all had the look of wandering ghosts.

Locally, only the Peach Village *Rulebook for Daughters* had the capacity to foster girls that sparkled like fresh flowers. Some said the manual was unfathomable, while others doubted its absurd legendary qualities, and some even questioned its very existence. For years the people talked, and its mystery grew deeper. A significant part of the Peach Village *Rulebook for Daughters* was devoted to the matter of abolishing tears altogether. The village mothers had struggled against tears for many years, a long tormenting process of probing into peculiar and secret formulas to make tears obsolete. They examined biological features, drawing on a host of human organs other than eyes as possible outlets, opening new avenues for discharge to the outside. Given the mothers' range of secret formulas, the girls had a wide assortment of tear-discharge methods, all of them strange.

Girls with large ears learned how to shed tears through them; the secret passage leading from eye to ear was thrown open for the flow of tears. A large ear is an ideal reservoir for tears; even the shallow ears of some girls discharged tears that wetted the neck, leaving the face dry. Girls with thick lips learned how to shed tears through them. Their lips were moist most of the time, rosy like the eaves of a house after rain; the overflow simply dripped to the ground without leaving a trace on the cheeks. With a mixture of envy and derision, people would say, "How lucky you are to cry like that, a drink of water right there at your lips, a veritable wellspring!" Most mysterious of all were the buxom girls, who actually shed tears through their breasts. The distance between eyes and breasts is so great that people from outside villages found this method virtually impossible to believe. "Peach Village girls' tears do indeed travel from eyes to breasts!" the local villagers would say. But, believe it or not, the virtues of breasts as conduits were openly proclaimed not by the women of Peach Village, but by their husbands. It was probably they who attested to the secret means of Peach Village girls to shed tears through their breasts, since those tears remained hidden in the inner folds of their clothing, suspenseful perhaps, but hidden.

All this brings us to Jiang Binu, whose name, Binu, meant Jade Maiden. She was a radiant young woman, blessed with fine features, whose tears should have been stored behind a pair of large dark eyes. Fortunate to have luxuriant long hair, which her mother combed into pretty buns behind her ears, she was being taught to hide her tears there. Unhappily, her mother died when Binu was still young, and her mother's secret formula died with her. Binu wept openly throughout her youth, keeping her hair from ever drying and making it impossible to keep the buns neatly combed. Anyone walking past her felt as if a rain-cloud had floated by, leaving drops of water in the air, which then landed on their face. Knowing that those were Binu's tears, they would flick away the liquid in disgust and wonder aloud, "How can Binu have so many tears!"

It would be unfair to say that Binu shed more tears than other Peach Village girls, but her way of crying was easily the clumsiest, and it was a characteristic of her pure innocence that she seemed incapable of devising for herself a clever way to shed tears. So, while the other girls grew up to marry men of commerce or landlords or, lower down the scale, carpenters or blacksmiths, Binu's choice was limited to the orphan Wan Qiliang. What did she gain from this marriage? A man and nine mulberry trees, nothing more.

Qiliang was a handsome, good and honest young man, but an orphan nonetheless, raised from infancy by a widower, Sanduo, who had found him beneath a mulberry tree. Local boys speculated that these two had fallen from the sky, that they were the sun and a star, or that they were birds or a rainbow.

"Qiliang," they would ask, "what are you?" He did not know, so he went home to ask Sanduo.

"You did not fall out of the sky," said Sanduo. "You were carried home from under a mulberry tree, so perhaps you are a mulberry tree."

After that, the boys all laughed at Qiliang, calling him a mulberry tree. Knowing that he was exactly that, Qiliang tended Sanduo's nine mulberry trees day in and day out, eventually becoming the tenth tree. The trees did not speak, so neither did Qiliang.

The others said, "Qiliang, you are a mute who is unwilling to learn a trade and knows only how to tend those nine mulberry trees. You cannot make a living that way, so one of these days you will have to cut down those trees for betrothal gifts, won't you? Who would marry you? Binu is the only girl in all of Peach Village who might consider it, because she is a gourd, and gourds hang from mulberry trees!"

So Binu married Qiliang; it was, it seems, the gourd's fate, and the mulberry's.

But it is common knowledge that, of all the males from Peach Village who died away from home, only Qiliang died in a place that was known to everyone in seven prefectures and eighteen counties, and that, of all the Peach Village women who were given to crying, only Binu's crying travelled far beyond the mountains. That was one of the great events in the history of Blue Cloud Prefecture, and the greatest moment in Peach Village's history of crying.

At noontime on the day of Qiliang's disappearance, Binu could cry only through her hair. She stood on the road gazing north, tears falling like rain from the buns behind her ears, wetting her green skirt. She saw Shang Ying's wife, Qiniang, and Shu's wife, Jinyi, who also stood on the road gazing north, grinding their teeth and clenching their fists; their husbands too had disappeared. Qiniang cried through her ears, from which a glistening tear drop emerged; Jinyi wept through her breasts, and since she had recently given birth to a son, whom she was suckling, the tears she shed were mixed with milk, soaking her silk clothes so completely that she looked as if she had climbed out of a water-filled ditch. On the afternoon of Qiliang's disappearance, a great many of Peach Village's men left without a trace, leaving behind wives, parents and children to tremble under mulberry trees.

Someone said to Binu, "The half-load of mulberry leaves that Qiliang had picked is still lying on the ground."

So she went to where the nine mulberry trees stood, despondent, and there she saw the basket of leaves. She sat down and began to count, but her count kept going wrong. Every spot where her hand rested, glistening drops of water rolled off the leaves and fell to the ground, for now her palms too were shedding tears. She carried the basket over to the silkworm shed, splashing water on the sun-drenched path as she walked. When she removed her shoes, she discovered that her toes were shedding tears as well, that they too had learned how to cry.

Now that Qiliang was gone, the silkworm shed seemed emptier than usual. Binu dumped the leaves into the silkworm pen, wetting it in the process. Worms that had not yet "climbed the mountain" scuttled out from under the covering, refusing to eat tear-soaked leaves. Overnight, many of the silkworms had climbed up onto hemp racks that Qiliang had made, but they stopped spinning silk, disappointed with the last basket of mulberry leaves their patron had picked, and longing for the life-giving promise of the spring baskets. Binu hung the empty basket from a rafter, from which beads of water now dripped to the floor. She spotted Qiliang's jacket, also hanging from a rafter and giving off traces of his sweat. One of his straw sandals lay by the silkworm shed door; she looked everywhere for its partner, but could not find it anywhere.

Binu walked slowly out of the silkworm shed, still searching for Qiliang's sandal; she searched from dusk till late at night, but found no trace of it. Refusing to listen to the counsel of others, she insisted that the sandal was hidden in the folds of dusk. The next morning found her pacing the ground beneath the nine mulberry trees; suddenly a straw sandal came sailing out of the Leng family mulberry grove on the other side of the road. The Leng family daughter-in-law cast a look of pity at her and said, "You can stop looking. Isn't that Qiliang's sandal?"

Binu picked it up and, after a mere glance, flung it back. "That rotten sandal? I don't know whose it is, but it isn't Qiliang's!"

The Leng family woman glared at her. "You're a girl who doesn't know what's good for her," she said angrily. "Has your soul fled just because your man is not at home? When a man leaves, his hands go with him, so do his feet, even that appendage between his legs is gone. So what good is a pair of straw sandals?"

Her face burning, Binu ran out of the grove onto the road, but even then she kept her head down, still searching for Qiliang's missing sandal, which hid from the sunlight, out of sight. Downhearted, Binu tramped up and down the public road leading out of the mulberry grove every day, always searching.

Villagers knew she was looking for the sandal, and, when they saw her, they pointed and said, "Qiliang took Binu's soul up north with him."

Chickens and dogs, not knowing what was happening, flew off or ran away when Binu drew near, hiding from the woman who stubbornly retraced her steps over and over. Even the roadside grasses acknowledged her sorrowful footprints: an invisible patina of tears overlaid each spot on the road where she had walked, and all the lush day-lilies and calamus along the way bowed down to her as she passed, piously proclaiming that, in their domain, there was no sandal here, no sandal here!

Binu searched for the missing straw sandal from summer to autumn, but did not find it. One day during the autumn she met a woman washing woven cloth on the riverbank. The woman told Binu that the cold weather would arrive soon, and that her children's winter clothes were not yet ready. Oh, how she wished she had another hand — one to wash clothes, one to make new clothes, and a third to mend old clothes. So Binu went down to the river to help. Yarn floated gently on top of water that had already turned cold, and as Binu held the still warm white yarn in her hands, she saw Qiliang's naked back in the autumn wind. "The cold weather sneaks up on you," she said. "They say that there, on the other side of Great Swallow Mountain, they feed people. But do they give them clothing as well? When Qiliang left, he was not wearing a shirt."

Washing the fabric also washed Binu's deepest worry up out of her heart and, with the coming of autumn, she was no longer seen on the road. The people of Peach Village heard that she had stopped searching for the missing sandal, and they assumed that a soul once taken from them had returned to the life of the village. Women came to Binu's hut, in part to share their thoughts on waiting in an empty house, but also to pry into her private affairs. With discerning eyes, they spotted traces of her tears around the stove and on the bed, and their noses picked up the bitter, sour scent of those tears, which spread through the room.

Without warning, a large drop of water fell from the thatched ceiling onto the face of one of the women. As she wiped the water from her face, she cried out in alarm, "Mother of mine, Binu's tears have flowed up to the roof!"

Another woman went to the stove and removed the lid on the cold pot, revealing half a pumpkin. She took a taste. Her brow crinkled. "That pumpkin broth has tears in it. It's bitter and sour. Binu, are you cooking this pumpkin in your tears? Whoever heard of such a thing?"

Standing in the rain-cloud of her own tears, Binu was wrapping up a large bundle. In it she had placed a finely tailored winter coat embroidered in a colourful pattern, a sash and a pair of boots lined with rabbit fur. That, the women thought, must be a bundle intended for Qiliang. Well, who wouldn't want to prepare a large bundle for a husband who had left home in such a hurry? They asked Binu how much the handsome coat had cost her, but all Binu could tell them was that she had traded away the nine mulberry trees, plus three baskets of silk from her cocoons and her spinning room.

The women shrieked in alarm. "Binu," they said, "how could you trade away nine mulberry trees, three baskets of silk and your spinning room? How will you live from now on?"

Binu replied, "Without Qiliang by my side, whether I live or die does not concern me."

Then the women asked, "Who are you going to get to carry that wonderful bundle to the other side of Great Swallow Mountain?"

"If no one else will take it," she said, "I will."

The women were convinced that Binu's mind had become confused, that she had no idea that Great Swallow Mountain was a thousand li away.

Binu said, "If I have a horse, I'll ride it. If I have a donkey, I'll ride that. If I have neither, then I'll walk. An animal can walk that distance. Are we not superior to animals? Who says I cannot walk a thousand li?"

The women, rendered speechless, ran out of Binu's hut holding their hands to their breasts, not stopping until they were well clear. They turned to look back at the quivering figure of the woman in the hut, and many of them felt a deep sadness. She may have stopped searching for Qiliang's straw sandal, they said, but her soul has not returned. One envious woman, wanting to hide her feelings, said cynically, "A thousand li just to deliver a winter coat? Does she suppose she is the only woman who loves her husband!"

Another woman could not really say if she had been struck by the power of emotion or if she had been stung by something Binu said, but she was no sooner out of the hut than her head began to ache. In order to dispel her mental and physical discomfort, she spat several times in the direction of Binu's hut. The others followed her example, and the noise drew a chorus of barking from the village dogs, who howled at Binu's hut all that night. Children got up out of bed, but were sent back, their little heads clasped firmly in their parents' hands.

"The dogs are not barking at us," the adults told them. "They are barking at Binu. Her soul left her the day Qiliang left."

Frog

Binu went to see the sorceresses of Kindling Village, bearing gifts, and told them of her plan to travel north to find her husband. She was anxious to know how to reach her destination before winter set in, so she could take him some winter clothing. The sorceresses revealed that they had travelled great distances north on spiritual wanderings, and one said she had used the feather of a crow as a compass. Every night she had roamed the three great cities of the north. Another said she had passed over North Mountain by hitching a ride with a caravan carrying tribute to the capital, secretly pasting a strand of her hair on the tribute chest, allowing her to watch the people feasting in Longevity Hall in the light of day.

The sorceresses cleverly avoided giving Binu an answer; instead, they examined her tongue and cut off a lock of her hair, which they held over a flame with a pair of tongs. She did not know what it was the sorceresses saw, but they knelt on a straw mat, placed bleached tortoise shells in an earthen vat, and then emptied them back out, all the time chanting incantations. Binu stared at their gaunt faces, their expressions a mixture of fear and joy.

"Do not go," they said. "If you do, you will not return, but will be struck down by illness on the road and die on the plain."

"Will I die on the way there," Binu asked, "or on the way back?"

The sorceresses blinked rapidly as they examined the pattern created by the tortoise shells on the mat. "Do you not fear death?" they asked. "Is it your wish that you will die on the way back?"

Binu nodded. "If I can deliver winter clothing to Qiliang," she said, "I will die happy."

The sorceresses of Kindling Village had never before met a woman like this. With censorious looks in their eyes, they said, "What sort of men's winter clothing is worth dying for?"

"Winter clothing for my husband, Qiliang, is worth dying for," she replied.

The sorceresses were speechless. Then, one last time, they placed the tortoise shells into the earthen vat and emptied them out onto the mat. They fell in the shape of a horse. "Since you are willing to sacrifice your life," they said, "then go. Do not forget that you must hire a Blue Cloud horse, for only a Blue Cloud horse can bring you back home."

So Binu went to hire a horse at Banqiao, only to discover that the domestic animal market there had closed down. An autumn flood had caused the river to overflow its banks and swallow up temporary bridges erected by the horse traders. Their riverside thatched sheds stood empty, and the fodder and the smell of livestock had drifted off on the wind, leaving only posts standing askew as they forlornly awaited the return of the horses, though indications were that they would not be coming back.

Water and straw merged to reclaim the riverbank and, in the wake of the plunder, Blue Cloud Prefecture was waterlogged and bleak. Binu stood at the water's edge, recalling how she and Qiliang had passed through Banqiao on their way to Cinnamon City to sell their silk. There had been many, many horses in the livestock market that day. The half-naked horse traders used to lead the animals down to the river to drink, all the while calling out to the women tending distant paddies, "Big Sister, Big Sister, come and buy my horse." That is what Binu had come to do, but traders from the Western Regions or from Yunnan were nowhere to be seen. All that was left of their presence was a large, cast-off, chipped vat in front of one of the sheds, filled half with rainwater and half with the remnants of burnt straw; a raven was perched on the rim.

Binu followed the riverbank, hoisting up the hem of her robe — pink flowers on a blue background — until she met up with the old pig tender, Sude, who stared at her in wonderment. "Are you trying to hire a horse? That, I'm afraid, is out of the question. There are so few of them left in Blue Cloud Prefecture that you could try for the next ten thousand years and not be able to hire one."

She walked on in despair, thinking of the sorceresses' prophecy, and was just stepping through a profusion of wild chrysanthemums when a frog hopped out from the water and, inexplicably, began to follow her. She stopped. "Why are you following me?" she asked. "You're not a horse and you're not a donkey, so go, go, go back into the water." The frog hopped back to the river, landing on a raft bobbing lightly on the surface. Someone had cleaved the raft in two, and the surviving remnant was rotting away, its wooden planks sprouting a bed of musky green moss that was home to the frog. Binu recalled how, during the summer, a blind woman had poled that raft downriver, wearing a bamboo hat on her head and the black attire favoured by women who lived in the mountains. As she sailed downriver she called out a name, but no one in the neighbourhood could understand her North Mountain accent. She was like a black egret that lived on the water, never on land. Eventually, the women who went down to the river to gather lotuses came to understand that the blind woman was searching for her son. But no one had ever seen her son, and nearly all the men of Blue Cloud Prefecture had been taken north as forced labour. Some people wanted to tell her that she should not be drifting downriver if she wanted to find him, that she should pole her raft up north. Others wanted to advise her that the first flood would soon arrive, making the river treacherous. But she stubbornly let the flow of water take her downriver, perhaps not understanding the language of those on the riverbank or maybe not knowing how to leave her raft; and she continued calling out for her son, first to this bank, then to the other. For the blind woman, the difference between day and night did not exist, so there were times in the dark early-morning hours when her shrill, mournful cries swirled above the riverbanks as her raft ploughed through, disturbing the crows in their treetop perches and interrupting the sleep of egrets on the sandbars. This night-shattering din startled people out of their pre-dawn sleep, the sounds from the river bringing them an indescribable sense of unease in the darkness. And their discomfort was justified: the autumn floods arrived early, and everyone said it was the blind woman who had set them loose. After the waters receded, there on the riverbank they saw the wooden raft, now torn in half. The raft was empty, the rafter gone, like a single drop of water in a surging river.

Binu had not expected that what awaited her at Banqiao was neither a horse nor a horse dealer, but a frog. It might well have been waiting there for some time, on the riverbank or in the water, listening for her footfalls, and the moment she left Banqiao, it began hopping along behind the terrified Binu on the road leading to the village. Was it in fact a reincarnation of the blind woman? All the women in Blue Cloud Prefecture had had previous lives, and some of those had come from the water. Wang Jie's voiceless mother, at one time an aromatic calamus, crawled down into a calamus thicket just before she died, and when Wang Jie ran up to the riverbank, his mother was nowhere to be seen. He could not tell which calamus plant was his transformed mother, so each year at Qingming, the day for sweeping graves, he went down to the river and performed the rites for all the calamus there. If someone could transmigrate into a calamus plant, Binu was thinking, couldn't the blind woman have transmigrated into a frog? She turned to scrutinize the frog, and was shaken by what she saw. The amphibian's eyes were like pearls, pure but lustreless. Yes, it was blind!

Hoisting up her robe, Binu ran like a madwoman and shouted fearfully, "It's her, it's her, she's come back as a frog!" No one was around to hear her — there was nothing but grass and weeds — so not a soul heard Binu reveal the frog's true identity. As she ran, she dimly heard the sound of wind coming at her from the river, carrying with it the mountain woman's cries for her son, and a sudden clarity in the indistinct shouts, "Qiliang! Qiliang!" Unable to believe what she was hearing, Binu slowed her frantic steps, then stopped running altogether. She stood still beneath a mulberry tree and thought about whether she should fear the ghost of a frog. She was not really afraid, so she resolved to ask the blind woman the name of her son. The frog hopped wearily toward her; it was indeed a frog, one whose blind eyes held the sorrow of the mountain woman, but its tightly closed mouth uttered not a sound about the life of the departed.

"What is your son's name? Is it Qiliang? I'm asking you the name of your son."

Binu waited patiently under the mulberry tree, until she realized that the frog was unable to answer this simple question. The villagers had said that people who live all year round in the mountains have no proper names and are either called by numbers or named after animals or plants. So the blind woman's son could not be called Qiliang. Remembering this lessened her anxieties, so Binu heaved a long sigh and, with her hands on her hips, looked down at the frog and said, "It's fine with me if you don't say anything. I know what you're thinking. You think I'm a raft, and you want to go with me to find your son! Well, you're quite well informed. The people in Millstone Village do not know that I plan to go to Great Swallow Mountain, but it seems that you know. My husband Qiliang is there, building a great wall. It is thousands of li from here. I am going there, even though I cannot hire a horse. But you, how can you get there? You could try hopping that far, but I'm afraid you'd be a cripple before you got there."

She had planned to hire a horse, or if there were no horses or her savings were inadequate to hire one, she would have hired a donkey. But, as it turned out, there were no donkeys either, and now it seemed that there was only this frog. What good was a frog to her? She could not, after all, ride north on its back.

Returning home empty-handed, she again met up with Sude and his pigs. He laughed when he saw her. "I wasn't lying, was I? All the horse traders were taken away in the summer, and no one can say whether they are men or ghosts today. How can you expect to hire a horse? You traded away your mulberry trees and your silkworms, didn't you? Well, if you have the money, why not hire one of my pigs? I'll show you how to ride it. Yes, hire one of my pigs."

Binu ignored the ravings of the pig herder and, with worry written all over her face, led the frog past Sude's pigs, sighing over her fruitless trip to Banqiao. With Qiliang gone, it seemed that nothing remained!

Clouds filled the Blue Cloud Prefecture autumn sky. Though weak and fragile, they rolled northward, passing over winding mountain ranges and abandoned groves of mulberry trees. Binu dreamed endlessly of Qiliang coming down the slope of North Mountain. Up in the sky the silvery Weaving Maid, Vega, was pointing the way home to Qiliang. Binu complained to people that she had seen him coming down North Mountain in the morning. "So why is he still walking when the sun drops below the mountain at dusk? Why won't he come down?" she said.

Someone answered, "You mustn't think such thoughts. You were having a bad dream. If Qiliang had come down the mountain in the morning, by nightfall his head would be rolling on the ground." They told her that all the Blue Cloud Prefecture men who had escaped from their labours in the north and come home had been caught and taken back. Their captors had then dug a huge pit on the other side of the mountain and buried the escaped labourers alive. With all those corpses down there, the people went on, it is likely that the mulberry trees on the back slope will grow tall and lush next year.

Qiliang had once said to Binu, "If you cross those mountains and pass through seven prefectures and eighteen counties, you will reach Great Swallow Mountain." But he had never told her how long that would take. As she walked along the riverbank on her way home, she gazed up at the far-off mountains, which appeared to retreat farther and farther into the distance the longer she looked. She wondered why there were so many mountains in Blue Cloud Prefecture, and could not imagine what a place without mountains might look like, what sort of world it might be. Many of the residents of her village had travelled to the plains and returned filled with envious stories of the splendour and richness of those places, whose residents did not, as foretold, have three heads and six arms, but were graced with the good fortune of vast land holdings. Binu had never seen a plain, and the people's descriptions of such places made her head spin. She was reminded again of the Kindling Village sorceresses' prediction, that if she did not hire a Blue Cloud horse, she would be struck down by illness and die on the plain. Who would come to bring her home? Would she die in a mulberry field or in an irrigation ditch, or would she die on a heavily travelled public road? Did people who lived on the plain grow mulberry trees? Did they grow gourds? If there were no gourds, there would be no one there to bring them home and, after she died, would she turn into a lonely wandering ghost?

Binu anxiously made her way home. At the village entrance, she changed direction and led the frog toward the nine mulberry trees. They had been submerged under the flood waters, yet all nine stood there calm and composed, looking as if they'd been planted in a paddy field. "You see how fine those nine mulberry trees are? Even after being under water, they're as good as ever," she said to the frog. "Those nine trees have fed vast numbers of precious silkworms, but now they belong to someone else." She waded through the water up to the largest tree and stood there, pointing to the gourd vines wrapped around the trunk. "See that," she said to the frog. "That is Qiliang and me: one is a mulberry tree, the other a gourd. You are the lucky one, your spirit can go wherever it wants on those frog's legs. Qiliang and I need a place where we can put down roots together. I'm not sure if mulberry trees grow up north, or gourds, and I wonder if there's place where we can settle down."

As she stood beneath the tree, Binu took one last look at the limbs and branches of all nine trees; seeing them was like seeing Qiliang. The image of him washing his face early in the morning materialized out of thin air as the sun was setting; though it was autumn, she could see him as if in winter. Though she had not been able to hire a horse, she saw him riding down the slope of North Mountain on a great Blue Cloud horse, wearing the new winter coat she'd taken him. How handsome and valiant he looked! Could there be another Peach Village man dressed as smartly? A blue cotton coat crafted by the seamstress from East Village, brocaded hemp shoes from Hailing Prefecture, and a phoenix-patterned sash that cost half a bushel of rice. The sash had a jade-inlaid hook on which he could hang anything he wanted.

Binu picked a gourd from the ground around the mulberry tree. Tears flowed from her palms when she did so. The tree and the gourd cried too, wetting her hand. The gourd had been taken from the heart of the mulberry tree, just as Binu had been torn from the heart of Qiliang. The vine was unhappy, the tree was unhappy and the woman was unhappy. But she knew that, whatever her feelings, the gourd had to be picked, for she needed to settle the matter of her reincarnation before she left. The sorceresses of Kindling Village had revealed another strange fate, and the memory of that dark prediction made her tremble with fear. "You were once a gourd," they cautioned menacingly, "so you should not casually leave the safety of your home. People are buried in the ground all over the world, but for you, Binu, no grave awaits. If you die in a foreign land, your ghost will turn back into a gourd, discarded at the side of a road, just waiting for a passerby to pick you up, cut you in half and give one half to this family, the other to that family, both of whom will throw you into a vat and use you as a ladle!"

Peach Village

Mud covered the ground in Peach Village, partially obscuring its boundaries. As the flood slowly receded, the unique circular huts of Blue Cloud Prefecture rose out of the water, each looking like half a human head embracing the joy of having survived a disaster. They appeared to be searching tirelessly for their owners, but the inhabitants, afraid of the water, were not ready to leave the temporary residences on the mountain slope to which they had fled. With their many silkworm racks, pottery, farming implements, and a small number of pigs and goats, they darkened the congested incline; exactly what they were waiting for was unclear — even to them — perhaps a total retreat of the water or perhaps just the passage of time. Time was now submerged in the water and would remain so until the water retreated. Only then would time be diverted to the leaves of mulberry trees and the white bodies of silkworms, and the innate rhythms of life would return to Peach Village.

The people on the slope watched as Binu returned with a gourd in her arms and a frog hopping along behind her. They laughed at the sight. "Binu, Binu, why are you carrying that gourd? Where is the horse you hired? And why are you bringing a frog home with you?"

Binu was used to being mocked by her fellow villagers, but the frog found the malicious attitude intolerable and bounded into a pond to escape. Binu continued to walk home again, alone now. As she passed unperturbed below the slope, lifting up her wet skirts with one hand and clutching the gourd with the other, she felt as if she were passing a grove of stupid mulberry trees. She could sense the biting, venomous glares of the young Peach Village women, who, now that autumn had passed, were no longer friendly and caring. Their men had all gone up north, leaving behind a lonely, empty village, and these women were faced with a cruel and unforgiving world. Binu had become used to living in isolation, and to the way the Peach Village women looked at her with cold, questioning eyes. The husbands of both Jinyi, a mushroom reborn as a woman, and Qiniang, who had come from pot ashes, had been taken the same day as Qiliang, yet these women were unwilling to travel north with her. Possibly, the prediction of the Kindling Village sorceresses had instilled in them a fear of dying on the road while searching for their husbands, and they were afraid of coming back as a mushroom or a pinch of pot ashes. Binu was unafraid. She had picked the last gourd from the mulberry tree and brought it home, intending to find a good spot to bury it and bury herself. Her lack of fear seemed to cast doubt upon Jinyi's and Qiniang's chastity and love for their husbands, inciting their wrath. So when Binu passed by Qiniang's shack, Qiniang came running after her to spit at her; and when Binu passed by Jinyi and smiled, she was rewarded with a spiteful glare and a contemptuous taunt, "Who do you think you're smiling at, madwoman?"

Binu ignored the hatred directed at her by others, because it was nothing compared with the love she felt for Qiliang. Back home she prepared the gourd for washing. First she removed the lid of the water vat; the ladle was missing. "Who took my ladle?" she shouted.

"The pig herder, Sude, took it," someone outside replied. "He said that, since you are going to Great Swallow Mountain, he would take your ladle for his own use. He would have an extra ladle for the house down below when he returns in a day or two."

"In that case, if he's so smart," said Binu, "why didn't he take my water vat too?"

The person replied, "Didn't you bring a gourd home with you? After you cut it in half and scoop out the insides, you'll have two more ladles!"

Binu refrained from revealing what she had in mind for this last gourd. Why should she, since they would only laugh at her, saying: Do you think that burying a gourd will save you? You'll still die on the road and be unburied! She bent over to check the pumpkins behind the water vat, and discovered that only two of the five remained. "Who stole my pumpkins?" she shouted.

"There's no need to say it like that," the person outside replied. "Stolen indeed! You are going to leave, after all. You can't eat all those pumpkins, and you can't take them with you, so why not give them away?"

After calming down, Binu moved the two remaining pumpkins outside. "I might as well put them out here myself," she said, "then you people don't need to continue being tempted by what belongs to me. Qiliang grew these pumpkins, the plumpest and sweetest in all of Blue Cloud Prefecture. Whoever wants to eat them, go ahead, but remember that they were grown by my Qiliang!"

After giving away her pumpkins, Binu had knelt on the floor and begun cleaning the gourd when a distant nephew, Xiaozhuo, whose head was covered with scabies, burst in through the door and shouted, "What do you think you're doing, madwoman?"

"I'm cleaning a gourd," she said.

"I see that," said Xiaozhuo, "but you're supposed to cut it in two and throw the two halves into the water vat to be used as ladles. So why clean it?"

"People have cut up all the other gourds, but this one is mine, and it will not be turned into ladles."

"What right do you have to let other gourds be cut in two, but not this one?" Xiaozhuo shouted derisively. "Is it the king of all the gourds?"

Binu said, "Xiaozhuo, have you forgotten that I was a gourd in a previous life? Haven't you heard that I am going to the north and will die on the road? Well, when I die, I do not want to be cut in two to float in other people's water vats. I must make myself clean and then bury my namesake whole in Peach Village. Once that is

31

done, I can set out with peace of mind and can save Qiliang from worries."

Sensibly Binu used the last remaining water in the vat, first to clean her gourd, then to wash Xiaozhuo's hair. However badly the boy treated her, she was, nonetheless, fond of him. But she could not stand his filthy head, nor its sour stench. When she finished washing his long hair, there was not enough water left for her to wash her own, so she dipped her comb in the little water that remained; but before she had finished combing out her hair, she ran outside, hairpin in her mouth, to see what time it was. The sombre look on her face gave everyone to believe that she was planning something. Later, when her neighbours recalled her final moments in Peach Village, they remarked that her immense calm had been more memorable than her madness. They watched her hair billow out like a black cloud as she led Xiaozhuo up the slope, dripping water along the way. She was still carrying her gourd, the top half covered by a not-quite-new silk handkerchief, a red thread pendant hanging from the bottom half. Seeing the villagers' disdainful gazes, Xiaozhuo wore a look of sheer embarrassment, but Binu held his hand tightly. "Madwoman!" he shouted. "Where are you going to bury that gourd?"

Binu gazed up at North Mountain, where her mother and father were buried. "I would like to bury it next to my mother and father but, since I am married to Qiliang, I belong to him and will not be able to attend to the Jiang family gravesite."

32

"Then why gaze up at North Mountain? Let's bury it in Qiliang's ancestral tombs."

"Qiliang is an orphan, like you. But you are better off than he is, because he has no ancestral tomb in Peach Village."

"So, where will you go?" cried Xiaozhuo impatiently. "Just find a spot anywhere. After all, you're burying a gourd, not yourself."

"Burying a gourd," said Binu, "is the same as burying myself. I need to find a good spot, a place with a tree, so that the vine can climb. It may be all right to suffer above ground, but not below. The terrain on this slope is high and dry, with daily sunlight, but too many people pass by; a wicked person might come along, dig up the gourd and make ladles out of it."

"Then bury it lower down."

Unsure what to do, Binu examined the slope. "This is no good either," she said. "It is where Sude lets his pigs feed, and if one of his rooting pigs were to dig up this gourd, that greedy Sude would take it home."

Xiaozhuo's patience had run out. "This place is no good, that place is no good, so forget about burying it," he said. "Toss it into somebody's water vat instead."

Binu pushed Xiaozhuo away in a fit of pique and walked the slope alone until she reached an old willow tree, where she saw the frog again. Now that Xiaozhuo was seemingly not around, it had returned, hiding timidly under the willow tree, thinking human thoughts. With the arrival of the frog, Binu once again saw the gaunt shape of the drowned mountain woman, dressed in black and wearing her straw hat. The woman was crouched under the willow tree waiting for Binu; the woman's ghost was waiting for her. Binu was able to see the ghost, because no one knows sorrow better than sorrowful people, and she felt a deep sadness for the mountain woman. Knowing how hard it had been for a blind woman to search alone for her son, Binu had sought a companion to travel north with her. The Peach Village women had avoided Binu and her idea like the plague. Even wild geese fly north and south in flocks, and anyone setting out on a long journey is on the lookout for companions. From summer to autumn Binu had looked in vain without finding a single one. Then along came the frog, which was not her ideal companion, but which she could not drive away because it was intent on travelling with her.

"You are too eager," Binu said to the frog. "How can I set out before I have buried my gourd? You are a frog, hopping from place to place in search of your son, and you are more fortunate than I am, because when I die I will become a gourd. If I do not bury myself, I will be left at the side of the road waiting for a passerby to find me."

The frog kept its vigil beneath the willow tree, listening intently to Binu's footsteps. Holding the gourd to her bosom, Binu took a turn around the willow tree. Towards the east, she saw a hillside covered with some waterlogged locust trees. Off to the west, she saw higher ground and an old juniper tree, the tips of its high branches ringed with an auspicious sunset. But someone had set loose a small herd of goats to graze there and, even if she drove them away, it was not the

34

right spot; the villagers could find her too easily. "Peach Village is so big, why can I not find a place to bury my gourd?" she cried.

Finally, she abandoned the search for the ideal burial spot of her imagination and, looking morose, turned her attention to the willow tree. "You'll do," she said. "You are not a shady tree to which people pray for good fortune, and I am not blessed with wealth and status, so neither of us can afford to be choosy about the other." She looked at the locust trees to the east and the old juniper to the west. "Let the others have their pines, their cypresses and their locust trees, I don't care. This willow is the one I want."

The young Xiaozhuo had by then climbed the heights of North Mountain to look down at Binu as she performed her solemn, secretive burial rite for the gourd. He had rich experience in burials: he had helped his father bury his grandfather, he had helped his mother bury his father, and finally he had buried his mother all by himself. Other youngsters would be interested in a gourd burial, but not Xiaozhuo — he had become too used to burying people. Nevertheless, he followed Binu's progress with keen interest.

Binu was crouched, busying herself beneath the willow tree, and when she stood up again, the gourd was nowhere to be seen. Cupping his hands around his mouth, Xiaozhuo trumpeted down the mountain, "Come and look. Binu has buried herself!" The words were barely out of his mouth when he choked on a gust of wind, which stopped him from revealing Binu's secret. It would be the last time he laid eyes on his aunt. Everyone, including him, had heard the prediction by the Kindling Village sorceresses that she was fated to die on the road. Xiaozhuo considered the spot beneath the willow tree a good place and thought Binu's choice of burial site was the only wise thing she'd done. On the day before she left Peach Village, Binu buried her gourd, and so buried herself in her hometown in advance of her death.

Bluegrass Ravine

The mountains around Bluegrass Ravine had been badly eroded by heavy human traffic, until what had once been a steep slope had been flattened out and become almost unrecognizable. The area was densely populated, and each gust of wind carried smells of fried cake and cow manure. It was one of Blue Cloud Prefecture's border regions. About thirty li away was the legendary Blue Cloud Pass, beyond which lay Pingyang Prefecture, a seemingly boundless expanse of cultivated flatland. People said that the King's horse-drawn carriages were speeding across that plain on a mysterious southern excursion.

Binu walked on until she spotted wheeled carts, which were drawn by donkeys and oxen, as the horses had all been consigned up north. Equipped with brass bells, they were harnessed to carts and assembled at the side of the road to wait for heavy loads. There in Bluegrass Ravine, the animals showed their diverse natures: the oxen, taken from dreary fields, loudly snorted confusion, while the donkeys, suddenly highly valued, voiced a kind of heady arrogance.

Countless box-like constructions had been put up at the side of a red clay road leading down the mountain. Binu could not tell if they had been built for royalty or wealthy gentry; it was the first time she had seen buildings like these. Flags hung from tall poles, most with a colourful word written on them. Binu could not read, so she asked one of the donkey-cart drivers what it said. Clearly he couldn't read either, for he stood there blinking for a moment, and then hazarded a guess. With a contemptuous glance, he said, "Can't read, is that it? I would say that the word is 'money'. What else could it be, since everything around here costs money."

Blue grass adorned the mountain pass area like gold dust. Even during times of war, it grew in crazy profusion, until it was said that Bluegrass Ravine flourished because of its special grass, gradually evolving into Blue Cloud Prefecture's most prosperous market town. As she made her way along the road, Binu met many women and children carrying blue baskets, and she assumed that they too were travelling north. "What would we go north to do?" they asked her. "It would be suicidal. No, we are on our way to Bluegrass Ravine to gather grass. Ten baskets of it can be sold for one sabre coin."

Binu looked around her and noticed a blue aura over the mountains; in the sunlight the blue grass was, truly, blue. The shabbily dressed grass-gatherers spread out and followed the stream, looking for thickets of grass, then eventually came together and, even though Binu was at the base of the mountain, she could see them up on the mountain fighting over clumps of grass. From a distance, the glowing fury of people scrambling on the mountain reminded her of wild animals fighting over food.

"Are you here to gather grass too? If so, why are you carrying a bundle on your head? And where are your basket and your scythe?" It was a donkey-cart driver in a green, turban-like headdress, a man of indeterminate age, with a bushy beard and unkempt sideburns. The look in his eyes was an uncanny mixture of evil and warmth.

"No, I'm not. I was told that there are donkey carts in Bluegrass Ravine that can take me north," Binu said. "Elder Brother, will you take your donkey cart up north?"

"To do what? Commit suicide?" the carter replied, cruelly. He seemed to cradle his hands, as if cold, and raised a bare foot. He studied the bundle on Binu's head out of the corner of his eye, trying to imagine what it contained. Then, without warning, he kicked Binu and demanded, "What's in the bundle? Open it up and let me see!"

"Why do you want to inspect it?" Binu asked as she lifted the bundle down. "You see," she added as she carelessly undid the wrapping, "it's nothing. It may look impressive, but it isn't worth much: just a winter coat for my man, and a frog."

"Did you say a frog? You're carrying a frog in that bundle?" The carter was flabbergasted. His eyes lit up like a lantern, and he started to go through the contents. "A frog, you say, well I'll have to see about that. Are you from Huangdian? Those people take a rooster with them everywhere they go, to lead the way. But a frog? How can a frog lead the way if you hide it in your bundle?"

"I am not from Huangdian, Elder Brother. I live in Peach Village, on the other side of the mountain. My frog is blind and cannot lead me anywhere. I must lead it."

"How can you say you're not from Huangdian? Your accent gives you away. You people are too sly to carry a bundle that is worth nothing. There must be a ghost in it."

Binu did not know how to prove that she was from Peach Village, but proving the innocence of her bundle was easy. Looking slightly offended, she shook it. "Come out here, frog, let our Elder Brother have a look at you. A ghost in my bundle? Never! A frog has nothing to be ashamed of. I'm not carrying any salt, they wouldn't let me. And I don't have a knife, you can't carry a knife in a bundle." Binu urged the frog to hop out and show itself, but it was curled up inside Qiliang's sandal, having got used to the warmth and darkness there, and refused to come out. A cowardly frog, it had been frightened all along the way, and now it was petrified. Binu explained the situation to the carter as she held the sandal out for him to see. "I'm telling you the truth, Elder Brother, there's a frog in there. What crime have I committed by taking a frog to Great Swallow Mountain?"

"Whether or not you have committed a crime is not for you to say. Your strange, furtive manner proves that you are from Huangdian! I'm telling you, the King has already arrived in Pingyang Prefecture, where people from Huangdian, and snakes, are to be eradicated!"

"I am not from Huangdian; I live in Peach Village. And this frog is not a snake. Please, look inside this sandal, and you'll see it's a frog, not a snake."

"So you refuse to admit that you're from Huangdian. The people of Huangdian have rebelled against the court for thirty years. Men and women alike have ventured forth as assassins and bandits. Who but a woman from Huangdian would travel from place to place alone, and who would hide a frog in a sandal? It is probably a dangerous frog, maybe a snake reborn in disguise! I'm telling you for your own good, if you travel beyond Blue Cloud Pass and reach Pingyang Prefecture, you'll see what's waiting for you. Snakes are the King's greatest fear. No matter how you raise them, they'll still bite you. And people from Huangdian are the King's mortal enemies. No matter how you deal with them, they will never submit. They are born with one thought: to assassinate the King. Let me remind you that all the grass in every town and village of Lulin Prefecture was burned, over and over, until every last snake egg was fried to a crisp. Anyone from Huangdian, young or old, is to be arrested and burned alive!"

That terrified Binu. She was not from Huangdian — which was on the other side of North Mountain — but she was frightened nonetheless. Her mind in turmoil, she clutched her bundle and walked to a roadside stand where straw baskets were for sale. People were staring at her bundle, so, with rising indignation, she showed

41

them Qiliang's sandal. "Everyone take a look. Is this a frog or is it a snake? Of course it's a frog, but he says it's a snake reborn as a frog." Their curiosity roused, people gathered round to inspect the frog and try to guess where Binu had come from.

"Carrying a frog or carrying a snake, what's the difference?" one of them said. "If this woman isn't a sorceress, she's a madwoman!"

In the prosperous town of Bluegrass Ravine, Binu discovered how it felt to be alone and forsaken. She did not know how to lie, yet the people refused to believe her. When she related her sad story, they doubted her from the very beginning. She told them she was from Peach Village, not Huangdian, that the two places were separated by a mountain, and that her accent was nothing like people from Huangdian. But the people in Bluegrass Ravine had no way of differentiating between the two accents, so they asked her, "The people of Peach Village, are they assassins, too?"

Binu told them she was the wife of Wan Qiliang. "Have any of you ladies and gentlemen seen my Qiliang?"

They laughed. "No one here knows your Wan Qiliang."

"Who is this Wan Qiliang?" someone asked. "Does he have his name tattooed on his forehead?" They told her that hundreds of thousands of workers were building the Great Wall, so who could possibly know anyone named Wan Qiliang?

Many of the people showed unusual interest in the bundle on her head, reaching out with dirty hands to

42

grab hold of Qiliang's winter coat. "Do you mean to say you're travelling all the way to Great Swallow Mountain just to give this to your husband?"

"Yes," Binu replied, "I'm taking him winter clothing. What else can I do? When my Qiliang was dragged off he wasn't even wearing a shirt."

It was a simple statement of fact, but the people treated it as the ravings of a madwoman or a dreamlike fantasy. Binu decided not to talk any more.

"You people won't believe anything I say, so I'm better off not saying anything," she muttered to herself as she painstakingly rewrapped her bundle. "If I pretend I'm a mute, you won't think I'm crazy," she said to the old man selling the straw baskets. "All I have to do to make you believe me is lie."

Looking at her out of the corner of his eye, the carter snorted and said, "Telling lies is hard for a woman like you. Not saying anything is even harder."

Binu had the feeling that this old man knew what was in her heart, but she was not about to appear weak, so she put her bundle back on her head and said, "How hard can it be to pretend I'm a mute? You say that not talking is hard; well, this time, I've made up my mind. You can all forget about trying to talk to me."

The carter leaned against his donkey cart and blocked Binu's way with his leg. It was a skinny, filthy leg that stuck out from under his fancy jacket, but it was more aggressive than an arm. He rudely but forcefully placed it against Binu's hip. "Leaving already?" he said. "Where to? I hear the sound of sabre coins in that bundle of yours. You're going to have to leave some as a road tax."

With a mixture of anger and shame, Binu pushed his leg away. Though she had vowed only moments ago not to speak, with his leg blocking her way, she had to say something. "What do you mean, a road tax? You're a highwayman, one who uses his feet!" She rubbed her cheek with one finger, trying to shame the man. "Elder Brother," she said, "I don't like to curse people, but that foot of yours is more obscene than other people's hands!"

He mocked her with a sneer. "I thought you were going to be a mute," he said. "Why are you talking?" He abruptly lifted his crossed arms out from his armpits and said "Hands? Hands are for fools. I've never touched a woman with my hands. Here, look for my hands. Where are they?"

Binu was astounded. There were no hands, just two stumps sticking up in the air, a pair of tree stumps flaunting their withered, severed stubs, the fingers and palms long gone. With a dreadful shriek, she covered her eyes. "Elder Brother," she asked, despite her fear, "who chopped off your hands?"

The carter deliberately displayed his handless stumps, first the left and then the right. "Why are you so interested in these? Thinking of marrying me?" He sniggered menacingly. "Who cut them off? Guess. I tell you, you can try till the end of time, but you'll never guess. I did it myself to avoid being taken to Great Swallow Mountain! First I cut off my left hand, but the pressgang man said that missing the left hand made no difference, since I could still carry stones with my right. So I asked my father to help me cut the right one off. I'll make your hair stand on end when I tell you what happened then. The pressgang messenger was outside pounding on our door while I was inside cutting off my right hand, but with my father's help both hands were gone just as he broke down the door."

"I can see that your hands are gone, Elder Brother," said an ashen-faced Binu as she peeked through the gaps between her fingers. "But how can you drive a cart with no hands?"

"I've got feet! Everyone in Bluegrass Ravine knows the carter with no palms. My legs and my feet are known far and wide by everyone except a stupid woman like you, who doesn't know what I can do with them. They are itching to put on a show." He raised them slowly, brought them together like a pair of hands, and clasped the reins between them. "I tell you," he said, looking Binu in the eye, "I'm a retainer in the employment of Lord Hengming, who would never have taken me on if I hadn't possessed the unique skill of driving a cart with my feet."

At a loss to understand the special status that the carter was boasting about, Binu's face wore only an expression of deep-seated fear, without admiration or respect. Apparently displeased, Wuzhang, or "No Palms", said, "What are you staring at? Is that pity I see? You pity me? You can keep your damned pity. If I hadn't chopped off my hands, I'd have been dragged off to Great Swallow Mountain to work like a slave. If I'd kept my hands, I'd never have developed the special skill of driving a cart with my feet, and I'd never have had a chance of being employed by Lord Hengming. Stop staring at me and look at that hunchback there with his oxcart. That hump did him no good, because they said it would have been perfect for carrying stones to the Great Wall. No need to bend over. The only way he was able to keep driving an oxcart in Bluegrass Ravine was to pay off the pressgang messenger."

Binu glanced at the hunchbacked oxcart driver, who was raking blue grass in his cart and sneaking looks at Binu and the palmless carter. Why, she wondered, was he smiling crookedly, salaciously? He laid down his rake when she looked at him, rested one hand against his belly, and blinked rapidly. "Is there something wrong with his eyes?" Binu asked Wuzhang. "Why does he keep blinking?" Wuzhang just laughed.

Then the hunchback became audacious; he slid his hand down into his pants and started making strange gestures. "How much?" he shouted.

Binu did not understand. "How much for what? I am not selling baskets."

The hunchback then made an obscene gesture with his fingers, the sight of which turned Binu's face scarlet. She turned and angrily banged her hand against her eyes, saying, "If all I see are people like that, what good are eyes?"

Showing no emotion, Wuzhang said, "Hit your eyes, go ahead, blind yourself. But then how will you get to Great Swallow Mountain? And, even if you manage that, with no eyes, how will you tell which one of the thousands of labourers is your husband? As a young woman alone on a long journey, remember that you wear your chastity on your sleeve. If a hen comes running out of the coop, you can bet there will be a rooster hot on her trail. The only way you will keep your eyes clean is, in fact, to go blind!"

Her anger mounting, Binu shrieked at Wuzhang, "If the world were full of obscene men like you, then being blind like my frog would be a blessing!"

The carters were clearly not good men. It was time for her to carry on through the pass and be on her way; she'd see what the wealthy people living up on the terrace were like, see if there were good people there. But was she going to walk straight past one man's donkey cart and another man's oxcart? No. Instead, she walked around the donkey cart owned by Wuzhang, who was patting his donkey lovingly on the rump as she went by. It was one of those light-coloured, long-and-low animals unique to Blue Cloud Prefecture. It was shod. As she passed by, grey droppings spilled out of its rump, immediately attracting a swarm of flies. Kind-hearted Binu tried to wave them away with her hand, a kindness that the donkey was not pleased to accept. Suddenly rearing up, it brayed in Binu's face, then edged its rump up beside her and let loose another burst of droppings. Even the Bluegrass Ravine animals showed her no respect, and yet she had a soft spot for this donkey; she could not help herself. Gazing into its big grey eyes, she said, "This donkey is better-looking than its owner. It's a good donkey, just slightly bad-tempered."

"I thought you wanted to go blind," the carter said. "You couldn't gaze at my donkey if you were blind, could you now? I'm telling you, you cannot gaze at my donkey for free. Every look will cost you one coin!"

"Let me ask you, Elder Brother. Which is more expensive, an ox or a donkey?"

"An ox is expensive, but a donkey is not cheap. More expensive than buying a person," the carter said.

Binu gazed timidly at the carter. "I know that livestock is expensive these days. If I cannot afford it, I won't buy. But I do have nine sabre coins. Would that be enough to hire your donkey cart?"

"So you are favouring me, are you? You want to hire my cart to take you up north, is that it?" Wuzhang glared at her before exploding in rage. "Don't you have ears? I told you, I'm in the employment of Lord Hengming. Weren't you listening when I mentioned his name? He is the King's brother! How else could I have such a fine cart? Bend down and take a look at this axle, at these wheels. Do you really think they are made for the likes of you? Take a look at the panther insignia on the canopy. That is Lord Hengming's insignia. Everything that carries this insignia belongs to him, including me. Do you understand? If not, take a look at the back of my jacket. See that, it's a panther insignia too."

Binu walked around the cart. A circled panther insignia was displayed proudly on the man's back. "I understand," she said solicitously. "You cannot hire the cart out because it does not belong to you. Then will you take me to see Lord Hengming, and speak to him for me? Ask him if he will let me hire the donkey. I wouldn't think of hiring such a fine cart, but if he'll let me have the donkey, I'll give him my nine sabre coins."

"Nine sabre coins, nine sabre coins! You think that carrying nine sabre coins makes you a rich woman, is that it?" Wuzhang made no attempt to hide his disdain. "If you possessed some unique skill, if you could fly up to the eaves or walk up walls, or if you breathed fire or walked on water, I would take you to see him, and he would reward me. If you could get your frog to wish Lord Hengming a long and happy life, I would take you to see him. Since a Huangdian rooster can lead the way down a road, a Huangdian frog ought to be able to speak. Have your frog say something to Lord Hengming, have it bow to him and wish him a long and happy life, and I'll take you to Hundred Springs Terrace."

"Where do you keep your ears, Elder Brother?" Binu said. "I've told you over and over that I am from Peach Village, not Huangdian. This frog comes from Banqiao, not Huangdian. It cannot bow, and it certainly cannot speak."

"If it can do neither of those, then you should not go. Not only would you fail to hire the donkey, but when Lord Hengming saw you, he might take a fancy to you. He has bought many women in recent years, some bright and beautiful, some broad in the hip, just right for bearing children, and some handy with needlework. He has kept some for himself and has given others to his retainers. Anything he likes, he buys. If you could cut up pieces of the sky and sell them, he would buy a big piece. Now, do you understand what my employer is like?"

Binu nodded at first but then shook her head. "You can say I'm from Huangdian all you want, but I'm not, and since I'm not, I'm not afraid." She looked at the resplendent donkey cart; and the more she looked, the more arrogant the donkey seemed, and the more luxurious the canopy seemed. She tried to imagine what the owner of that cart might be like, but her mind failed her. She sighed and gave up trying. "Elder Brother, that must be a rich and powerful man whose donkey cart is better decked out than any person could be. Well, I am not interested in hiring that donkey. My feet will take me to Great Swallow Mountain. But I don't understand why everyone I meet along the way lies to me? They all tell me that Bluegrass Ravine sells large livestock."

"That just shows how stupid you are. Large livestock means people, not animals!" Having lost his patience with her, Wuzhang picked up a whip with his feet, raised it high and brought it down with a crack right above her head. "Go on, get out of my way. I'm here to take on a new retainer for Lord Hengming. He'll be coming down the mountain any minute now, so stop bothering me."

Binu jumped in alarm, the violent movement causing something metallic in her bundle to clink.

The carter's eyes lit up. "You're not a woman who lies," he said. I can tell that you do in fact have nine sabre coins. Well, I didn't lie to you either. Go and buy a head of large livestock. Go out of this pass and look down the mountain. You'll see a place where they buy and sell people. Large livestock is all you'll find there."

The People Market

It was nearly time for the people market to close for the day, now that the sun was setting, but people still lined both sides of the street, the most notable being a cluster of bewitching young women. Given their dazzling, elaborate dress, they had probably come from the northern districts of Blue Cloud Prefecture. Rouge covered their foreheads, cheeks and lips, and they were dressed in colourful blue, peach-red or pastel-green dresses. The sleeves and hems were adorned with diamond patterns, some large, some small; their sashes, decorated with inlaid stones of agate and strips of jade, were tied in butterfly knots, and on the ends hung jade rings, silver lockets or perfume sachets. It must have been their splendid attire that lent them such self-assurance and a palpable sense of pride. Their faces betrayed little sadness over the chaotic state of the world around them. It was late in the day, and potential buyers had yet to show, so the women chattered like birds about to return to their nests for the night, making a racket over one thing or another. Scattered around them were barefoot mountain women in bamboo hats, and a few middle-aged women from a distant prefecture, all wearing simple dark clothing. They stood silently, with downcast looks that befitted their station, as they gazed at horse-drawn carriages travelling up and down the road. Across the way, elderly men and boys sat lazily, cross-legged, several of them asleep, with their heads resting on their neighbours' shoulders. One boy, unmindful of his station, had climbed a date tree by the road and was shaking the branches with all his strength, even though the dates had been picked long ago; all that fell to the ground were dry dead leaves.

A man sitting beneath the tree shouted, "Stop that! You'll kill the tree that way, and there won't be any shade left. Then you'll have to stand in full sun waiting to be sold, and sooner or later that will kill you."

The threat worked on the boy, who stopped shaking and sat still in the fork of the branches, from where he spotted an unfamiliar woman with a bundle on her head coming down from the mountain pass. A new target had presented itself. Reaching under his shirt, he took out a slingshot and shouted excitedly to the people below, "Here comes some new large livestock! Hand me some stones, hurry!"

The others watched as Binu, with a bundle on her head, walked under the tree; the women across the street heard the stones bombard her body, but Binu merely looked up into the branches of the tree and said, "You cannot hurt me with your stones. But you had better be careful up there or you might fall and hurt yourself." Her warning caught the boy off-guard; he put away his slingshot and said to the man under the tree,

"I hit her with my slingshot but, instead of scolding me, she cautioned me to take care not to fall out of the tree. The head of this large livestock has a problem."

Binu stood fast on the dirt road. Since the tree and its surroundings were men's territory, she could not stop there. But across the road were all those women, whose fancy dresses rippling in the desolate autumn breezes struck her as somehow improper. So she stood in the middle of the road and took a good look at the Bluegrass Ravine people market. The finely attired young women were, at the same time, sizing her up.

"Why is she carrying a bundle on her head? Isn't she afraid of crushing her hairstyle?"

"Hairstyle?" one of them sneered. "It's a rat's nest, that's what it is. Southern women don't fuss over their hair."

Another woman's attention was drawn to Binu's face. With a combination of envy and ignorance, she said, "I didn't know there were beauties down south too. Just look at her delicate moth eyebrows, her phoenix eyes and her willowy waist, a classic beauty."

A woman beside her added caustically, "Too bad she never learned how to wash her face or apply make-up. She's actually smeared dust all over her face in place of rouge. Look at the dirt on that face; you could plant crops in it."

Binu was not immediately offended by the malicious gossip. From Peach Village all the way to Bluegrass Ravine, she had believed that women who congregated at the side of a road must be waiting to be taken to Great Swallow Mountain, and she expected to meet

54

women from other towns who were also searching for their husbands, assuming they could travel north together.

She walked up to a woman in green who was eating flatbread. "Are you waiting for a ride?" she asked. "Are you going to Great Swallow Mountain?"

The woman looked at her out of the corner of her eye. "Great Swallow Mountain?" she replied, still munching her food. "This is not a stopping point for labourers heading north, so how could there be any rides to Great Swallow Mountain? If you want to go there, you'd best get back on the road while it's still light."

"Then what are you all waiting for? And where are you going?"

The woman in green removed a packet from her sash and waved it in front of Binu. "We're not like you. See that? It's an embroidery kit. We are not large livestock, we're skilled needleworkers who are waiting for a carriage from the Qiao family textile mill to take us into employment. Why are *you* standing here?"

Noting the derisive tone of the question, Binu said, "You shouldn't talk like that, Elder Sister. None of us chooses what we are. Just because you can do a little needlework there is no reason to act like spoilt girls. In Peach Village girls grow up knowing how to plant mulberries and raise silkworms. Our needlework may not be as fancy as yours, but every thread in that packet comes from a silkworm. I can tell that your silk threads came from Peach Village silkworms."

The woman blinked. "Are you saying our thread is silk from your hometown? Are you from Peach Village? No wonder you sound like crackling thunder when you speak!" She laughed smugly. "I know who you are. People say there's a madwoman in Peach Village who is afflicted with lovesickness. She is carrying a frog with her as she travels north to search for her husband. It's you!"

Binu was shocked to learn that news of her travels had reached Bluegrass Ravine. It did indeed sound like news of a madwoman. She detected a look of pity in the eyes of the woman in green, the controlled pity of a normal person towards a mad one. "Who is spreading such vicious rumours behind my back?" she said. "I am taking winter clothing to my husband. That is not being lovesick, and I have no affliction. Any woman who could bear to let her husband go shirtless in winter is the afflicted one."

"If you have no affliction, then hurry up and get back on the road, deliver your winter clothing, go all the way to Great Swallow Mountain. If you don't hurry, you'll arrive after the winter snows, and your husband will have become a snowman!" The woman cackled over her little joke and then, with a swish of her sleeve, edged closer to her embroidery sisters.

Binu heard the gleeful sounds of the woman passing on the news: "Can't you see who that is? Come take a look, it's the madwoman of Peach Village!"

The whispering embroidery women turned to give Binu looks of timid curiosity. "It's her. Yes, it's her. The lovesick one. The madwoman. What about the frog? It's hidden in the bundle on her head." Caught in the needlesharp gaze of the women, Binu felt her face and body prickle all over. Worn down physically and emotionally, she lacked the strength to reason with the women. It was just like Peach Village, with girls chattering away whenever they got together, and they loved spreading idle talk about her.

All this time, the mountain women stood quietly at the edge of the people market like a row of shadowy trees in the settling darkness. Binu left the gaggle of decked-out embroidery women and walked up to a woman in black who was holding a conical hat in her hand. She was reminiscent of the mountain woman on the raft and reminded Binu of the frog in her bundle. Binu thought of asking the woman if she was from Northeast Mountain and, if so, if she knew a woman who poled a raft to search for her son. But the hostility she had experienced in this people market had destroyed her confidence in human contact. So she chose to say nothing. I ask you nothing, and you ask me nothing, she thought. Binu stood silently amid the mountain women, waiting with them for carts and horses to pass by.

The woman in black lowered the hat that she held in front of her face, revealing ashen, swollen features. The moment she opened her mouth to speak, a rank, fishy smell engulfed her. "You ought not to stand with those women. But then, only the aged, the ugly, the sick and dying, those with no skills, should stand here with us." The woman, with a blank look on her face, eyed up the bundle on Binu's head. "You are better off than us," she said, "since you at least own a large bundle. We have nothing and can only stand here and wait. We are not waiting for a cart from the textile mill. If someone were to buy us to pull a plough, that would be enough. We are what is known as large livestock. But no one wants to buy mountain women like us; they think we are too ugly and too stupid. We will never find a cart, so we stand here awaiting death. If that is what you are waiting for too, then stand here with us."

Obviously, there was no place in the Bluegrass Ravine people market for Binu. She could stand with neither the embroidery sisters nor the mountain women. Unable to see an alternative, she stood in the middle of the road to wait, like the others; just wait. The last cart passed by the people market; the sky above Bluegrass Ravine darkened slowly, winds from the mountain were chilled. Every now and then, a cart passed down the road, creating a stir among women on both sides of the road. The embroidery sisters brushed and straightened their clothes and waved their colourful packets, retaining a modicum of reserve. The boys across the street simply ran over and grabbed hold of the cart canopy, hoping to jump aboard, but were driven back by the driver's whip. "We're not buying people, not today," the driver said.

The mountain women chased meekly along behind the cart, shouting, "Don't you want some large livestock? We don't need wages, just some food."

The man on the cart answered, "No, we don't need large livestock, not at any price."

With the bundle still resting on top of her head, Binu moved out of the way of the cart. The sight of her solitary, impoverished presence once again captured the attention of the boys under the tree, who began pointing and gesturing at her bundle.

"Let's see if there really is a frog in that bundle," one of them said.

Another voice, gravelly, like that of an old man, responded, "See if there's a frog? What in the world for? Let's see if there are any sabre coins."

It was becoming clear to Binu that the people market was a dangerous place, especially as night was falling; the middle of the road was not a good place for her to be loitering. She was about to move to the left side of the road when the date tree rustled noisily and the boy with the slingshot jumped to the ground. At the same time, one of the other boys stood up and headed straight for Binu, who screamed, "What are you, bandits? If you're not careful, the authorities will arrest you and take you away!"

That stopped them in their tracks, but the gravelly voice began again, this time with a sinister edge, "Let them. In jail they'll have to feed us, and that is surely better than starving here!"

That comment energized the boys. "Let them take us away, that way they'll have to feed us!"

His friend tried to act like a highwayman. "Pay a road tax before you can leave!"

The boys rushed at Binu like wild animals. She screamed and sought help from the fancy women across the street, shouting out, "Are you going to stand there and let them rob me?"

The women glanced indifferently at her. One of them, in a blue dress, pointed to the other side of the road. "That's their grandfather sitting there. If he doesn't care, why should we?"

Binu turned and grabbed the sleeve of one of the mountain women, who immediately pulled back.

"Don't grab me, run away! You're asking for trouble, standing here in the people market with such a big bundle on your head."

With no choices left to her, Binu took off, running.

At that moment the frog chose to show itself. People on both sides of the road were shocked to see flashes of light above Binu's head, when the already legendary frog appeared miraculously, as if it had fallen from the heavens, and landed softly on top of Binu's head or, more accurately, on top of the bundle. The darkening sky above Bluegrass Ravine made it difficult at first for the people to see the frog clearly, but its tightly shut eyes and the silvery flashes of tears around them put fear into everyone, for no one had ever seen a frog cry.

"Don't touch it, it's a poisonous toad! You'll go blind!" came a loud and frightened warning from the old man beside the road. "Stay clear of that woman, she's a sorceress, for sure."

The boys backed off in the direction of the tree. "Didn't you hear Grandpa say it's not a frog, that it's a poisonous toad?"

"Why is she taking a poisonous toad with her?" the slingshot-boy asked.

"Grandfather told us: she's a sorceress. Let's get out of here!"

They ran to the tree for protection, and Binu shouted at the boys' backs, "I *am* a sorceress! And I have a poisonous toad. If not, how could I deal with the likes of you in my travels? How could I get where I'm going without this poisonous toad?"

Binu had salvaged her dignity in Bluegrass Ravine thanks to a frog that could cry. Even though it was unexpected, it was the sort of dignity worthy of a true sorceress. As she tidied up her bundle in the fading light, her body emitted an aura of mystery. The fancy women reacted by gathering round her, followed by the guilt-ridden mountain women, who fell in behind. The occupants of the people market — women and children, young and old — were like fish in treacherously shallow water schooling towards the mouth of a spring; they swam towards Binu, embracing the natural respect of a fish to water. They wanted her to tell them their destiny. Binu felt uneasy, and she was anxious to remove herself from their midst. But then she was reminded that they too were poverty-stricken, people to be pitied, and that they shared a similar destiny. Binu had never known a life of fine clothes and good food, but was well acquainted with one of cold and hunger. She had never met anyone reborn from dragons or phoenixes, but had seen a great many humble people who had emerged from earth and water. What then could be so hard about predicting humble destinies? Taking courage from this thought, she looked for a clean patch of ground, on which she laid Qiliang's sandal; after reinserting the frog in the sandal, she copied the behaviour of the Kindling Village sorceresses by drawing a circle in the dirt and sitting inside it, lotus position.

The woman in green offered her the uneaten half of her flatbread, curtsied and said, "Forgive me, I could not tell that you were a sorceress. My husband was taken off to Great Swallow Mountain in the summer, and I have received no word from or about him since. Please make a divination for me; ask your frog if my man is still alive."

With a sideways glance at the woman's fancy dress and adornments, Binu reached out and touched the sash, on which jewels and pieces of agate hung. "You are dressed so beautifully, while your husband has been left shirtless. When the northern winds begin to blow, I am afraid he will not survive."

"Will he freeze to death?" the women asked in unison.

"No," Binu replied. "The frog says he will die of a broken heart."

The shocked woman in green pleaded, "What can I do?"

"Go home and find your husband's warmest winter clothing. Lay it out in the sun tomorrow, and once it is aired and fresh, you can deliver it to Great Swallow Mountain in person."

The woman hung her head in shame. "I no longer have his winter clothing," she said. "I traded it for a bag of grain. I am not your equal. You are a sorceress who can fly across mountains and walk on water. I cannot travel such a long distance, I am much too frail. If I tried, I would die along the way for sure."

"You are afraid of dying along the way, but not afraid that your husband might freeze to death, is that what you are telling me?"

The woman in green had no answer for that, but before long began to speak in her own defence: "He is suffering, but my days are not pleasant either. What good is it to be a talented embroiderer? Isn't it the same as waiting here for death to claim me? In any case, I was a butterfly in my previous life, and that is what I will return as. Then I can fly to Great Swallow Mountain to see him."

A hunchbacked old man with a white beard walked up and handed Binu a sour date. Breathing heavily, he said, "My son was on his way down the mountain with kindling to sell when he was taken. The villagers falsely accused him of stealing a goat, for which he was arrested. I went to the county government office, but was driven away with a beating. The yamen officials said that, even if he *had* stolen a goat, they had no time to arrest him. Please, Elder Sister sorceress, ask your frog if my son actually committed a crime, and tell me where they have taken him."

"Your son has committed no crime," she said, "and he has certainly been taken to Great Swallow Mountain to work on the Great Wall. It is the hardest, most exhausting labour in the world. The men of Blue Cloud Prefecture fear hard, exhausting labour less than anyone else in the world, so they have all gone to Great Swallow Mountain."

For a brief moment the old man seemed consoled, but then he asked, with a heavy heart, "How many days does it take to travel from Bluegrass Ravine to Great Swallow Mountain?"

"The frog says that by foot it will take until the onset of winter."

The old man succumbed to despair. "Then I will not be able to go. If it were a matter of a few dozen li, I would go with you. But walking makes me breathless, and I could never walk that far. If only I were ten years younger, I'd travel to Great Swallow Mountain, even if it killed me. I would take my son's place there. But I will soon be laid to rest, and can only wait here, one tormenting day after another, until I see my son pass by. But then, I am afraid that I will already be in my grave and, if he walks past, I'll not be able to see him!"

The effect of the words "Great Swallow Mountain" on the people was for a moment like rubbing flint in their eyes; but the sparks were soon extinguished by the wind. Binu alone was willing to travel to Great Swallow Mountain, and even the frog's tears lacked the power to persuade the others into travelling with her. For them, waiting by the side of the road was the better choice. The sluggish crowd had abandoned all but the act of waiting. When the mountain women began to weep and wail, the winds from the mountain pass turned unbearably cold, and Binu knew more clearly than anything that, in this forlorn people market, only she held out a bit of hope. She was destined to be alone.

The fancily dressed embroidery sisters asked about their fate, and for each of them it was one of anguish, one of longing and worries, never one of health and happiness; their faces told of their displeasure, and they began to doubt and question the truth of the frog's tears and Binu's sorcery. They left the people market, making their way noisily to their homes in the nearby valley. The destitute and homeless mountain women also left, dragging their weary bodies back to hastily dug burrows that offered meagre protection from the elements. After peeling back the dead branches that covered the openings, they crawled in like rodents. But, before she entered her burrow, the woman in black turned and waved to Binu, warmly inviting her to bed down with her for the night. Binu graciously declined the offer. These women had grown used to living like rodents, content in their burrows, but not Binu. She was used to walking above ground during the daytime and, when the moon and stars shone through the darkness, she was not afraid to walk at night.

Binu stood alone in the wind, gazing down the mountain road, which blurred into darkness. She heard the tinkle of a bell in the distance, and a moment later saw the familiar carter, the one who drove with his feet. His cart cut through the darkness towards her from the mountain pass, but was slowed by Binu's abrupt move to the centre of the road. Wuzhang lashed out with his whip to get her to move, but to no avail; he was forced to stop.

"You haven't managed to get yourself sold, I see," he said. "Try again tomorrow. But for now get out of my way. Our new retainer was late. We have already missed Lord Hengming's party."

Without a word in response, Binu stood her ground and reached into her bundle to take out a shiny sabre coin, which she held out towards the man's feet.

"Have you really become a mute? Say something. Just where do you want to go?"

"I cannot stop, Elder Brother, I must keep going. Be a good man and take me part of the way. So long as I'm heading north, I'll go as far as you'll take me."

He reached down with his foot and deftly picked up the coin with his toes. He raised his other foot and shook it up and down. Binu did not know what that meant. She paused for a moment, but then took out another coin and placed it between his toes. Her hand trembled visibly. "I've never spent so much money before," she said. "If Qiliang knew, he'd scold me severely. All that just for a ride. But I have been on the road for three days and nights, and tonight I cannot walk another step."

"You think I've asked for too much? Don't you realize whose cart this is?" The carter turned to look at the new retainer seated behind him, who answered his gaze with a small movement of his head. "This brother is a kind man. Without a nod from him, I could not take you anywhere. Hurry up and thank him, for you will be riding in Lord Hengming's cart, and for only two sabre coins. Few people have that good fortune."

Binu bowed to the man and climbed into the cart. The new retainer was a giant of a man who cast an enormous shadow. In the little light that remained, she saw the tangled hair that hung to his shoulders, and noticed that his face was covered by a dark kerchief. His body gave off a slightly musky odour.

"Where are you from, Elder Brother?" Binu asked timidly.

The man appeared not to have heard. But Wuzhang spun around and bellowed, "No talking! I never ask where my passengers are from or where they're going. How dare you ask such questions!"

The mysterious stranger said nothing and, as Binu rode along, she felt as if she were sitting next to a large boulder. She tried hard not to disturb him, but the bumpy ride occasionally made her bundle brush against his jacket, causing the frog inside to croak, and croak again. So she took it down and held it in her lap. And as she did so, she noticed smudges on the man's boots, although, in the darkness, she could not tell if it was mud or blood. She moved a little farther away from the man thinking about the dreadful places her travelling companion might have come from. An unintended glance at the eyes glimmering above the dark kerchief revealed a glint of arrogance or hatred. Or was it sorrow?

Hundred Springs Terrace

In the soft moonlight Hundred Springs Terrace loomed up like a bright, lush island. With its high terrace and soaring eaves, its candles flickering amid stringed and woodwind music, it looked like the last giant beast in a moment of rapture. The driver brought the cart to a halt at a riverbank, turned to Binu, and said, "Get off, get down off the cart. I've driven you twenty li for your two sabre coins. It's time for you to be on your own again."

Binu did not hear the carter's command, so intent was she on avoiding the eyes of the man whose face was covered. Twenty li of travel had exhausted her. Her companion's cold demeanour and the way he kept his hand under his robe, as if he had a sword hidden there, had reminded her of a man from Huangdian she had encountered on North Mountain as a child. As he roamed the mountain with something under his arm, the children of Peach Village had run after him to ask what he was hiding. "What's that under your arm, Uncle?" The man had smiled and opened his coat. It was a bloody human head! The thought of that human head had kept Binu from looking at the man's robe and, as the cart bumped along the road, she had felt herself floating in the evening air.

The carter kicked her roughly. "Are you deaf or have you fallen asleep? We're at Hundred Springs Terrace, so get off, and don't let anyone see you!"

When Binu climbed down from the donkey cart, she felt the ground beneath her feet shift; having trouble keeping her balance, she crouched down in this alien, dreamlike place. Hundred Springs Terrace was separated from the woods by a moat that surrounded it like a silken sash. There were glimpses of human figures on the other side, and a row of lanterns with panther insignias flapped in the wind. Then the sound of chains and a winch rose together, and a giant drawbridge rumbled down from the sky next to the terrified Binu. She jumped to her feet. "Elder Brother," she shouted, "you cannot leave me here. You accepted my two sabre coins, but only took me twenty li. You must return one of the coins to me."

The carter and his passenger turned to look. The passenger remained silent, his eyes still shining brightly. "Do you want me to take you into Hundred Springs Terrace for your two sabre coins?" the carter asked. "Open your eyes and take a good look. Does this look like a place for you?"

Binu held her breath as she listened to voices coming from across the moat. "You're lying, Elder Brother. Who says a woman can't cross that bridge? I hear women's voices over there."

He laughed. "Those are pleasure women. Want to join them? You've got the looks, now all you need to do is learn to sing and play an instrument, and you might pass. Give me another one of those coins, and I'll introduce you to a pleasure house. You can be one of the women then."

Before Binu could say a word, the frog began to fidget. It had hidden shyly in Qiliang's sandal all the way to Hundred Springs Terrace, but now it boldly jumped out of the sandal and landed on the back of Binu's hand, stopping just long enough to leave a blistering mark, before hopping off. Shocked by the sudden movement, Binu watched the frog hop around in the moonlight, all the way up and onto the donkey cart. From the way the retainer shifted his body, she could tell that the frog had hopped into his lap.

"Don't go there, that is not your son!" Binu shouted fearfully, suddenly realizing what the frog was thinking. "Come back here! He doesn't know you; he is not your son!"

Binu's shout was unfortunately too late. The man grabbed the frog, and Binu saw his hand flick in the air, sending a tiny black object arcing into the water.

A furious beating of gongs came from beyond the drawbridge. It was a sentry signalling to the donkey cart to hurry up and cross over. The carter raised his feet and snapped his whip in the air as Binu ran to catch up. In a panic, she grabbed hold of the retainer's sash; without thinking what she was saying, she screamed out to the man, "That was not a frog, it was your mother's ghost. You will be punished for flinging your mother into the water!"

70

The man stood up; something glinted under his coat, and in one fearful instant, his sword had severed his sash where Binu's hand was clutched. The carter's enraged voice came from behind, "What do you mean, his mother? A ghost?" He roared at Binu, "Be careful he doesn't bury that sword in your heart! He's a master swordsman, Lord Hengming's newest retainer. His weapon recognizes no one; not family and certainly not ghosts!"

Binu sat down hard, still clutching a piece of the sash. On it was the panther insignia and splashes of something dark; this time she was certain it was dried blood.

The cart crossed the drawbridge, and the bridge rose into the air and disappeared from view, leaving Binu stranded on the opposite bank. The human figures that had been visible in the lantern light were also gone; all that remained were the red flames flickering beneath a cauldron. Every so often an attendant emerged from behind the wall to add kindling to the fire. Binu stood beside the moat, the retainer's sash still in her hand, and gazed at Hundred Springs Terrace, bathed in moonlight, still looking like an enormous beast and filling the sky with a mysterious scent that could have been its breath.

Binu walked along the bank, searching for her frog. A clump of duckweed floated on the surface of the water, which rippled in the moonlight. Riding on top, heading towards Hundred Springs Terrace, was a tiny dark object that left little ripples in its wake. It had to be the frog, the pitiful ghost following the trail of its son. An uproar of men's voices emerged from a tent across the water; maybe they were all the sons of the woman in black, but who among them would recognize or acknowledge a mother who had been reborn as a frog? Binu waited by the moat for a while, certain that the frog would not look back. Binu had lost her travelling companion and would have to walk the rest of the way alone.

Now that the frog was gone, Binu's bundle was silent and Qiliang's sandal was empty. She washed it in the moat, then gazed at her reflection in the water. The moonlit surface was smooth as a mirror, but still she could not see her face; it was absorbed into the glittery water. Unable to see her reflection, she suddenly forgot what she looked like, and when she tried to recall her appearance, the images that came to her mind were of a wizened old mountain woman on a wooden raft, and a tear-streaked face with inauspicious colouring. She knelt by the water and rubbed her eyes, recalling how bright and beautiful they had been. But her fingers, strangers to those eyes, were driven away by an assault from her eyelashes. She then felt her nose. The women of Peach Village all envied her dainty, well-shaped nose. But it too rebuffed her touch with indifference, even releasing a bit of snot onto her fingers as an added display of mischief. She dipped her fingers in the water and rubbed them across her lips, recalling that they had been Qiliang's favourite feature; he had told her often how red and sweet they were. Now they were tightly compressed, rejecting the water she brought to them. All her features seemed to be upbraiding her. "You have forsaken everything, including your eyes, your nose and your lips, the totality of your beauty, all for Wan Qiliang."

Binu could feel the sticky dust of spent tears when she touched her hair, and she realized that she had not washed it since leaving Peach Village. So she removed the hair ornaments and plunged her black tresses into the moat. Even with her face lying right up against the surface of the water, she still could not see her reflection. Little fish swam up to her, for they had never before seen a woman performing her toilet in the moonlight, and they thought that her hair was a new kind of water plant. They began to nibble passionately on her floating hair. Binu wanted to see what the little fish looked like, but Qiliang's face emerged from the water and she felt his nimble fingers stroking her hair in the water, out of sight. She could not recall what she looked like, but Qiliang could never be forgotten. She remembered how his face glowed in the sunlight beneath the nine mulberry trees, filled with optimism and ardour; in the dark, however, he was like a little boy, childish, bashful and occasionally a bit morose when he thought about what the future might hold. She remembered his hands. In the daytime they were coarse and strong, ideal for handling farm tools and tending the mulberry trees; but when he came home at night, her body became his mulberry tree, and the sweetest harvest began. When he got too rough, she slapped his hands, and they deftly moved on. When his hands became tired, she slapped them to bring them back to life, more passionate than ever, more daring. Binu missed Qiliang's hands, missed his mouth and his teeth, missed his mud-caked toes, missed that special part of his, which was sometimes wild and unmannerly, at other times fragile and needy. It was his second son, the secret one, one that rose in the night to light up her dreary body, bit by bit. She recalled how Qiliang's body emitted scorching hot sunlight in the dark of night, and this indelible memory illuminated the dark sky above the strange land around her; it also lit up the road north. Binu got to her feet beside the moat and gazed along the road to where a forest grew; she knew that the one and only road leading to the north was hidden among those trees.

Binu started walking and soon came upon a ragged array of thatched huts deep in the forest; some were tall, others were squat, but they were all dark, and they shuddered in the night winds, which carried towards her the stink of human and animal waste, and the snores of exhausted sleepers. A lantern hung outside one of the huts, and Binu wondered if that might be Lord Hengming's stable. Guided by the light, she approached the stable and peered in, only to find it empty, except for three horses eating hay from a trough; their silvery manes radiated a noble, somehow watery light in the darkness. As she pushed open the door, a shadow flashed before her eyes, and something made of metal captured her hand and held it secure. It was the hooked end of a scythe. When she recovered from the shock, she saw an old groom, naked from the waist up, hunkering down in a dark corner; the scythe was his.

"I've told you people you are not allowed in the stable. The next time I catch you I'll treat you like a horse thief." He made a gesture of drawing the blade of the scythe across his neck and sneered maliciously. "Anyone who tries to steal a Hundred Springs Terrace horse pays with his life!"

"I'm not trying to steal a horse," Binu protested. "I was just passing by."

"This forest belongs to Lord Hengming, and this is not a public road. Who gave you permission to come this way?" The groom glared at Binu. "Eight or nine out of every ten people who pass by here are assassins. If you're not careful, the authorities will seize you and cut off your head!"

"I am not an assassin, I am from Peach Village." Binu took advantage of the thin light cast by the lantern to look closely at the groom's face. "I can tell from your accent, old man, that you are from North Mountain. Do you know a man from Peach Village by the name of Wan Qiliang? I am his wife."

"North Mountain, where's that? And who is Wan Qiliang? I cannot let you into the stable, no matter who you know. The White Dew period has arrived, and these horses will go into town to deliver Hundred Springs elixir. If something happened to one of them, my head would be on the chopping block!" An inquisitive look flashed across the old groom's eyes as he spoke. He stepped out from behind the door and poked at Binu's bundle with his scythe. "I can see you came with no weapon. What are you, a woman alone, doing in the forest at this late hour?"

"Old man," Binu replied, "I hadn't planned on entering the forest. I am on my way north, and this is the only way I can get there."

"Everybody else heads south. Why are you heading north? Even men dare not head north. How does a mere woman have the nerve to do so?" The old groom held up a torch to see Binu's face, filled with doubts as he took her measure. "I can see you are a pretty thing, and that you have a solid-looking bundle, but I cannot be sure if you are a person or a ghost. They say that most pretty things that travel at night are, eight or nine times out of ten, ghosts. These old eyes can't be sure." He began to mumble pensively. "I'm old and don't much care what you are. I'll assume you're not a ghost and urge you to find a safe place to spend the night. I cannot let you stay here, though, and you must not seek out a goat pen or pig sty. They smell bad and the men who tend them would not let you out of their clutches, whether you are a woman or a female ghost. I recommend the deer shed. The youngsters who tend the deer are orphans and have nearly become deer themselves. A woman is safe with them."

So Binu went to the deer shed, outside of which a sleepy-eyed boy was just then relieving himself, scratching himself with one hand, peeing with the other. From where she stood in the dark, she saw that a small gourd hung from the boy's neck and that a pair of strange deer horns poked out from the hair stacked on his head. But what truly startled her was that his stream of urine headed straight towards her feet, like a river finding its way to the ocean. When she moved to the left, it followed; she moved to the right, and it veered towards her, a bright ribbon of liquid that seemed to seek her out. She held her hand over her mouth, so as not to frighten the boy, and ran over to a haystack.

Too late, he spotted her and screamed, "A ghost! A ghost is hiding in the haystack!"

From behind the haystack, Binu said, "I am not a ghost. I am a woman from Peach Village." But before she could explain herself further, a swarm of boys burst out from the deer shed.

"Bring a torch!" One of the boys shouted. "Ghosts are afraid of fire."

"Be careful you don't start a fire," another boy said. "Lord Hengming would make you very sorry. Go and get clubs. Everyone go after the ghost with a club!"

Binu knew she was cornered. She stepped out from behind the haystack and, attempting to smile, she asked, "Have any of you children ever heard of a ghost travelling with a bundle on her head? I am not a ghost. I am from Peach Village, on my way to Great Swallow Mountain. I am the wife of Wan Qiliang of Peach Village."

In a tone that sounded worldly-wise, one of the boys asked, "Who is Wan Qiliang? I know every one of Lord Hengming's retainers, and none of them is called Wan Qiliang."

A bright-looking boy demanded, in a high-pitched voice, "Prove that you are not a ghost. I heard the wind follow you when you walked."

"That was the sound of my clothing. I eat in the wind and sleep in the dew, and I have grown thin. My clothing now fits much too loosely and, when I walk, the wind blows through it."

The boy with the gourd hanging from his neck had been staring at Binu's bundle, curious about its contents. "Ghosts sometimes travel with bundles on their heads, and they are filled with human bones. You say you are not a ghost; then throw your bundle over here and let me check for human bones!"

His friends applauded his suggestion. "Quickly, throw your bundle over here," they said.

Binu backed away, shaking her head and clutching her bundle to her. This only increased the boys' curiosity. "Search it!" one of them shouted. "Search her bundle." Dark figures were already advancing on her before the sound had died out. Then the boys rushed at her, and she saw in their movements the bounding gait of deer.

With the smell of deer in her nostrils, Binu shouted in desperation, "There's a poisonous toad in my bundle."

They stopped in their tracks, the way a deer stops when it hears a whistle. They understood the threat posed by a poisonous toad. "Liar!" they cried out. "Only a sorceress travels with a poisonous toad."

"I *am* a sorceress," she said.

One of the boys, sensing he was being tricked, said to the others, "First she's a ghost, then she's a decent married woman, and now she's a sorceress."

Another demanded proof. "You say you have a poisonous toad. Well, call it out, we're not afraid!"

"I am not lying to you," said Binu. "My poisonous toad is right now in the moat around Hundred Springs Terrace, searching for her son."

Binu had lost herself in her own explanation. As she glanced first to one side and then the other, the boys saw through her bluster. They cupped their hands beside their cheeks, and bounded deer-like towards her, their eyes on the bundle she was carrying. Though they were mere boys, and stick-thin at that, they had no problem wresting the bundle away from Binu and ripping it open. The five hidden sabre coins in the secret compartment of the winter coat were scattered on the muddy ground, extracting excited whoops from the boys. Binu watched as Qiliang's winter coat flew through the air like a startled, panicky bird, then settled on the ground, where it was seized by multiple pairs of hands. Some fought over the sleeves, some the flaps. Qiliang's padded cap wound up on one of the boy's heads, only to be snatched away by another and pulled down tight. Qiliang's sash snapped crazily in the air.

Binu shrieked at the top of her lungs and watched as the shrill sound of her voice made the stars above the treetops shift in the sky. That one shriek was all she could manage. It followed Qiliang's winter coat, which flew from one boy to another, while her body slumped to the muddy ground; she was kneeling before the boys, but to no avail, for they leaped across her shoulders and over her head. She struggled to her feet again, but that too was futile, for she was too slow to catch boys who ran like deer. Their bare legs bounded through the forest; they were swept up in a carnival of wild pleasure.

79

With her last ounce of strength, Binu grabbed one of the boys by the leg.

"You cannot take my bundle from me. Heaven will strike you dead!"

But her words were swallowed up; the leg in her grasp had a trick to play. The boy let her hold on for a moment before nimbly leaping out of her grasp, leaving only a proud laugh from its owner as he disappeared into the darkness.

Binu could not see her bundle anywhere; she saw only the stars shifting in the sky and forest shadows swaying in the dark. She bent down and prayed before the darkness, whether to heaven or to earth, to the boys or to Qiliang, she did not stop to choose. But before she heard a word of her own prayers, she fell unconscious to the ground.

Deer-boys

The boys dragged the sleeping Binu over to the goat shed, waking the goatherd, who picked up a club to prepare himself for whatever was coming. But he threw down his club when he saw Binu, tossed his head back and laughed. "I thought you'd caught a wild deer," he said. "Instead you've brought me a human captive, and a pretty young thing, at that." He tried to send the boys packing, but they refused to leave their prey.

"You stinky goatherd," they said, "we know what's on your mind, so don't get any ideas. We bagged this ghost, and we haven't questioned her yet."

The goatherd gazed longingly at the woman in the haystack. Examining her hair, her earlobes and her pulse, he announced confidently, "She has a pulse and her ears are warm. She's a woman, not a ghost."

One of the boys walked over, unhappily dragging the bundle wrapping behind him, "There's no toad, and no tortoise shells," he said. "Not even a rooster bone! She lied to us; she's no sorceress."

"There's only one way to tell," said the goatherd, "and that's by touching." He thrust his hand under Binu's coat, capturing the bawdy attention of the boys, who ran up to watch and laugh. "This is nothing to make a fuss over," he said. "Haven't you ever seen how Lord Hengming inspects his women?" He kept his hand under her coat, trying to look solemn. "You don't know," he said, "but there are men out there who dress like women to save themselves from being conscripted; since we don't know where this one came from, I need to find out if she's really a woman or not."

Binu's dust-covered robe was ripped open, and the goatherd clutched her pale breasts. "These are fine examples," he said, "shaped like bowls. Lord Hengming says that women who have never nursed have bowl-shaped breasts. Come, look closely. Don't they resemble bowls?"

The boys gathered round the haystack, somewhat hesitantly. "They don't look like bowls, they look like steamed buns," one of them said.

That gave the goatherd an idea. His eyes lit up. "Well, then, want a bite? Come, come, take a bite!"

A boy was forced down on top of Binu and, as he struggled to get up, his ear pressed against her breast, and that side of his face was immediately dampened by a bitter liquid. His eyes burned, and he heard an unearthly sound. He raised his head quizzically, grabbed hold of his own ear and shook it, then bent down to look at Binu's breast. A shocked cry burst from his mouth: "Come and listen, it's crying! Those are tears!"

All women cry, but the boys found it hard to believe that an unconscious woman could weep through her breasts, and so they wanted to believe that the liquid was milk. But when they thought back to their childhoods, they recalled that milk is white and sort of sticky, not translucent. One boy suggested that the liquid must be sweat. But on such a cold autumn night, when not even thick hemp cloth could keep a person from shivering, how could she release so much sweat, especially since she was half-naked?

The goatherd dipped his finger in the liquid oozing from Binu's breast. He tasted it and spat it right out. "It's bitter, worse than the bark of a tree. Have any of you ever tasted someone else's tears? Come over here and taste this, and tell me if it's tears."

The boy with the gourd around his neck stepped out from the crowd and leaned against the haystack to lick one of Binu's breasts. He nodded with certainty.

"They're tears," he said, "a woman's tears." In the midst of looks of doubt and suspicion all round, he was calmly self-assured, perfectly willing to swear that these were uniquely feminine tears. He told the goatherd that, the night before he left home, his mother had wept as she held him in her arms. Some of her tears had slipped into his mouth; just like these, they were bitter and pungent.

The goatherd's lustful smile of pleasure froze on his face. He pulled his hand away from Binu's body and said with horror, "This woman must be one of those weepers from the south. Anyone who encounters one of them will never again be happy in this life." He flung his hand in the air as a nameless terror passed before his eyes. He turned to the boys. "You have a nerve," he shouted, "dragging this unknown woman all over the place in the middle of the night. Who told you to bring her to my goat shed? Get her out of here this minute!"

The boys pitched in to lift Binu up. She was wet from head to toe. By this time they were utterly convinced that what had flowed from her body was a strange kind of tears, for not only had they tasted them, but they'd examined them with their eyes and ears as well. They had felt strong movements within those breasts, something akin to sobbing, and enraged cries. With trepidation, they stole a closer look at her inviolable breasts; their faces expressed the awe and veneration they felt for them. Beyond that, the weeping breasts presented them with a puzzling question, which prompted a debate. They knew of brutal men who had torn off their mothers' clothes in the fields beyond the village or who had disrobed their sisters. Why were these other women's breasts so reconcilable? Why did these mothers and sisters not weep through their breasts? Someone suggested that this woman was different from the others, that so many men had abused her that she had cried until her eyes were dry, forcing her tears to flow from her breasts. What about her hands and her feet, could they cry too? On the recommendation of the boy they called Chancellor Deer, they carried Binu over to the chicken coop, laid her out on top of it and began a close examination.

One of them removed her tattered straw sandals. "She's walked so far her toes are blistered," he reported. "But no liquid."

Another held Binu's hand and scrutinized every inch, front and back. "Her hands are like those of a corpse," he announced. "Ice cold."

Chancellor Deer said unhappily, "Shake her hand, wiggle her toes, see if any tears come out."

The two boys followed his command. As they did so, fear crept across their faces, and a rooster inside the coop began to crow in response to the commotion outside. Streams of tears began to flow from the blisters on Binu's toes, and the palms of both hands were suddenly awash.

This enigmatic, sorrowful being inspired the boys to whoop and cheer with raw delight. When they had calmed down, they began to see more possibilities. They had discovered hidden treasure in the person of a woman who happened to pass by. Each had thoughts of his own, and none could tear himself away from Binu and return to the deer shed to sleep. The boy with the gourd around his neck reminded the others that it was he who had discovered this mystical woman. They kept watch over Binu, respectfully, greedily, as if she were a living gold mine.

With the confused crowing of the rooster as a backdrop, they debated how best to profit from their captive. Someone — it was hard to say who — suggested selling her to the vaudeville troupe in Cotton City. His suggestion was rejected by General Deer and Chancellor Deer: General Deer said the person who had made the suggestion was stupid. "The purpose of a vaudeville troupe is to make people happy. Why in the world would anyone buy a woman so that people could watch her cry?" Chancellor Deer said that if they were going into business, they should go the whole way. Lord Hengming has said, he told them, that all special people and other treasures should be presented to Hundred Springs Terrace, and that the donor will be well rewarded. He said that Lord Hengming kept more than nine hundred retainers. Some were gifted with talents useful in an emergency. Others were expert musicians, chess masters, calligraphers or artists. There were also assassins and executioners, as well as clowns who could change their faces at will; but a retainer who could shed tears through her breasts, the palms of her hands and her toes would hold special appeal for Lord Hengming. This suggestion met with unanimous approval from the boys. The only possible problem was that Binu was a woman. There were many women in Hundred Springs Terrace, but they were either part of Lord Hengming's family and entourage, or singing girls and pleasure women. The boys were not confident that Hengming would accept a woman as one of his retainers.

With Binu still lying there unconscious, the boys discussed the best way to present her to Hundred Springs Terrace before Lord Hengming went out for his morning hunt. If he accepted her, they were assured a generous reward. They did not want pork, or sabre coins; what they wanted was admission into Hundred Springs Terrace to become Lord Hengming's horse-men. They knew of lucky deer-boys before them who had entered Hundred Springs Terrace to become horse-men, and even though it was the lowest of the low among the retainers, a status that did not permit them to eat or travel with Lord Hengming, it was nonetheless a sure-fire means of having food to eat and clothes to wear, and an absence of worries. It was the life they longed for, and this unconscious woman might well have brought good fortune with her, good fortune that had fallen out of the sky onto their heads. With hope alive in their faces, the boys strapped Binu to a wooden plank and set off for Hundred Springs Terrace.

The Drawbridge

"We caught a weeper! Here comes a weeper! Here comes a weeper!"

Across the moat, the drawbridge maintained its silence amidst the boys' shouts, the shrill cries of a herd of deer. Eventually the noise attracted the attention of a pair of bridge workers. But no matter how beguilingly the boys described the mystical Binu, a woman who could shed tears from all parts of her body, the workers not only refused to lower the drawbridge but also called the deer-boys all sorts of names, saying that they were more stupid than real deer. Besides, a weeper? So what! They lowered the drawbridge for galloping horse-men, for bird people who sang so beautifully, and for people whose faces always wore beaming smiles. But the bridge was off limits to a weeper. An elderly bridge worker came out and gave the deer-boys some good advice: no matter how wide a net Lord Hengming threw for great talents from all over the world, he would never accept a weeper — someone who simply cried, and cried, and cried — as one of his retainers. A woman's tears would destroy the *feng shui* of Hundred Springs Terrace. He also took the opportunity to complain about the decline of public morals: "Every waif and stray is intent on entering Hundred Springs Terrace as a retainer," he said, "so they can eat for free. Even a woman who can do nothing but weep thinks she can enter Hundred Springs Terrace!"

But the deer-boys, still holding Binu up in the air, refused to leave. In high-pitched voices, they argued their case as they saw it: "Plenty of women who can only sing or dance are allowed into Hundred Springs Terrace, so a weeper who can shed tears through the palms of her hands and her toes ought to have immediate access."

The bridge workers laughed. "What do you children know? Women are allowed into Hundred Springs Terrace because they're good at laughing, not good at crying. If a woman wants to make Lord Hengming happy, beyond singing, dancing, giving pleasure, or entertaining with special skills, there are plenty of other things she can do, things you will never understand."

Bewildered by the man's comment, the boys tried harder to convince him. "Come, see for yourselves. Her hair is saturated with tears. Her toes and hands all shed tears."

One thrust his hand in and squeezed Binu's breast to taunt the bridge workers. "Come and look at this. Even her breasts can shed tears!"

The frantic slaps had awakened Binu, only for her to discover that her clothes had been pulled back to expose her breasts. After all the hardships she had suffered, her dust-covered body had been bared by a bunch of curious deer-boys. Their brutal probing, imitating deer behaviour, was worse than being robbed. She felt a subtle pain in her lower abdomen, and one of her exposed breasts was shedding tears of shame. She was virtually drowning in tears. Her bundle hated her: "Such clever hands, and you can't even keep hold of a simple bundle!" Her breasts resented her: "All those clothes wrapped tightly around your body, and you let those boys touch us with their filthy hands." She heard the boys call her a weeper and wondered if she had shed all her tears while she lay unconscious. Tied fast with ropes, she could sense how light she had become; it was as if her body, overcome with shame, was trying to detach itself from her. As she came to, she gradually realised that, while in her mind, she was still on the road, her exhausted legs were refusing to do her bidding. She knew that her trek had been interrupted, and that in the process she had lost her bundle, and that falling unconscious at the height of her torment had brought a taste of tranquillity. In the midst of that strange tranquillity, dream-like, Death itself had come calling; a gourd had fallen through the darkness, sending splashes of tears into the air, and she had seen herself in death. A person holding a gourd to his chest had stood in mid-air as dawn was breaking, and she could not tell if the gourd was leading the person, or if the person was taking the gourd along. She could not see clearly, but she knew it was Death, and that Death was waiting for her.

Her mind cleared into the realisation that she had not even managed to leave Blue Cloud Prefecture, and now she was going to die. She recalled the prediction of the sorceresses in Kindling Village. They had said she would die on the road, and she had been prepared for that. "If that is the case, so be it! I am bound to meet up with a decent person sooner or later, and I will beg that person to deliver my bundle to Qiliang," she had said, thinking that then she would die happy. But seeing Death so early in her travels had caught her by surprise and made her wonder if she would die at the hands of these boys. She looked up at the stars. A few of the boys' heads bent down over her, blocking out most of the sky, and she could feel their hot breath on her face. She heard them cheer.

"She's awake. The weeper is awake!"

Binu detected the gamey odour of deer. Death had placed itself among these boys, and she struggled to recognize it through the barrier of her dream. Who had been holding the gourd in the dream? Starlight danced on the boys' faces. Which one of them was Death?

"I am going to die soon, so untie me and find me a gravesite facing the sun, where you can bury me," she begged them. "I'm better off that way, since I can no longer continue on this tortuous road. Plant a gourd vine over my grave. When Qiliang sees it on his way home, he'll know it is me. And, even if he does not see it at first, the vine will spread out across the road and trip him up. Then he will know."

The deer-boys stared down at the tied-up Binu and cried, "No one is going to bury you. You're a weeper." But her eager acceptance of death puzzled them, so they talked among themselves again, trying to decide if she was mad. All of a sudden, Chancellor Deer shouted across the moat, "The weeper is dying. If you don't hurry up and lower the drawbridge, you'll miss your chance to see her tears." That shout elicited no response. The deer-boys cast their eyes towards the drawbridge, their patience exhausted. It was not coming down.

"Open your eyes and see where you are. This is Hundred Springs Terrace," General Deer yelled at Binu, "not a place where you can dig a grave wherever you please. Lord Hengming rides his horse past this spot every day."

"Then carry me over to the moat. Lord Hengming rides on a road, but surely he cannot ride on water. Throw me into the water and watch me sink below the surface. If a gourd rises to the surface, then I will be dead. That will make things easy on you and on me."

"Who would dare throw you into the water? That moat belongs to Lord Hengming, it is Hundred Springs Terrace's royal canal, and corpses are not allowed in it. Cleanliness is essential to Lord Hengming. Did you notice that not even a dead chicken or rat floats in that water? A human corpse would be unthinkable!"

"Then carry me over to the road, find a spot where the dirt is loose, and I will bury myself."

"You are not an earthworm that can wriggle its way underground. You cannot bury yourself."

"You offer me neither a road to life nor a path to death. What are you going to do with me?"

The deer-boys were at a loss as to what to do with their catch. They put their heads together for a long time, until General Deer solemnly announced to Binu where she would spend the night. "Lord Hengming will not take you, so we will carry you to our Deer King. Hundred Springs Terrace may not want you, but our Deer King will, for certain!"

The Deer King's Grave

They carried Binu deep into the forest, where, apparently, the Deer King lived.

Binu begged them to let her down off the wooden plank. "I won't cause any trouble, and I won't try to run away," she said. "After all, I'm going to die whatever I do. Please put me down and let me walk. The only things that are tied up like this are beasts on their way to the slaughterhouse."

There was a moment's silence, then a chorus of, "No, you are a sacrificial offering, and they are always tied to a board."

Soon they arrived at a little earthen mound: Deer King's grave. Sacrificial offerings were piled in front: an ox bone, a brass lock, a seashell, a slingshot and some dried-up dead birds. A tall scarecrow wearing a cloak of tattered palm-bark stood at an angle beside the mound, an arrow in its hand. Apparently, it was the keeper of the grave. But now that they had Binu, the scarecrow was knocked to the ground, where General Deer stamped on it, saying, "You failed to watch over the Deer King's grave. See how birds have eaten the grass around it?"

General Deer took out a chain and told the deer-boys to release Binu from the wooden plank. Before she could even move her legs, one of the deer-boys roughly wrapped the chain around them and chained her to a tree. General Deer heard her cry out. "Don't be afraid," he said. "This chain allows you to walk ten paces, enough to reach the edge of the forest to pick wild fruit. Don't use Deer King's grave as a toilet. Use the forest. Chancellor Deer will be nearby to help you. There are wild boars in the forest. Don't let them root around the grave, don't let birds land on it, and don't eat all the wild fruit you pick; leave some as sacrificial offerings."

So this was the place the boys had picked for her. She was afraid, not of dying, but of this bizarre spot. She began to scream and struggled madly against the chain that bound her. But she was quickly surrounded by the deer-boys, who pinned her down with their thin but powerful legs and stopped her struggling.

It occurred to Binu that they weren't children after all, but a real herd of deer. Or if they weren't deer, then they had the hearts of deer. She was frightened, not of deer, but of their deer hearts. A human heart can move a human heart, but how was she to move the hearts of a herd of deer? She shouted loudly, calling out Qiliang's name. The mournful sound sent evening dew falling to the ground. Her cries made the leaves and branches fall and curl, but the boys' callous hearts remained unmoved.

General Deer gave her a disdainful look. "Is Qiliang your husband?" he asked. "What good can calling his name do? If he came, we'd chain him to the tree next to you."

Binu stubbornly continued to call out Qiliang's name, and she heard the old elm tree behind her shout, "Qiliang! Qiliang! Qiliang!" Then a crisp sound resounded in the night air: the branch of the elm tree snapped in two and crashed down on top of General Deer.

With a convulsive shudder, he threw off the offending branch and cried out in alarm, "What is this woman shouting?" he demanded. "Her shouts have snapped a branch!"

Chancellor Deer picked up the branch and examined the dewdrops that covered it. "Shouting didn't break it, crying did. Her tears are all over this branch."

At that moment, the boys were plunged into inexplicable terror, from which emerged the certainty that they must stop the woman from shouting. Her shouts were so shrill that they swirled around the forest, just as their mothers' cries had when they were calling their sick children's spirits back from the mountain. Binu's shouts had opened the door of their memories; they found themselves thinking back to their mothers, wherever they were, and that led to thoughts of their homes, and from there to those wretched virtues they detested — conscience, filial piety, moral integrity, all things that were anathema to free-ranging deer-boys. To stop those memories, they had to stop Binu shouting.

Chancellor Deer picked a strip of hemp from the grave and stuffed it in Binu's mouth. "Go ahead, shout," he said. "I'll just stuff the hemp in tighter." Dew from the elm tree rained down on Chancellor Deer, who complained loudly that his deer horns hurt terribly and were about to fall off. General Deer stepped away from the tree, protesting that when he had stepped on a fallen leaf, sharp pains had shot up his leg, and that several months of practising how to leap like a deer were about to be cancelled out in a single day. The other deer-boys had suffered a variety of uncomfortable reactions. The hand of one still meandered about his own chest, as if seeking the location of his heart; a tear had appeared in the corner of another's eye.

Now that they had silenced Binu, the boys appeared to recover and bounded away. They stopped after a few leaps, turned and studied her face closely, anxiously waiting for something to happen. With her voice stilled, her eyes became a latent danger. They were opened as wide as they would go, the pupils reflecting the semi-darkness of the pre-dawn morning, empty, it seemed, of all traces of resentment or anger. They reminded the boys of their mothers' eyes, although Binu's eyes radiated a watery light, an obvious sign that tears were about to spill from them. Tears from her breasts, the palms of her hands and her toes had surprised and delighted the boys, but tears from her eyes threw them into a panic.

"Tears! Tears! There are tears in her eyes! Don't let her look at us. Cover her eyes!"

They rushed up, tore off Binu's sash, and wrapped it around her eyes, but that had no effect on her tears, which flowed down her cheeks like a river, crystal-clear drops that splashed lightly onto the boys' faces.

Troubled by a nagging premonition that Binu's tears were imbued with evil curses, the boys tried to get out of the way, leaping and screaming and wiping the tears off, but it was too late. They all experienced an attack of sadness, accompanied by powerful feelings of homesickness — a faraway village, a dog, a pair of goats, three pigs, crops in the field, the indistinct faces of father and mother, sister and brother. All these thoughts made noisy incursions into their storehouse of memories. The horns on their heads fell away. They held their noses and covered their eyes, but it was too late: a rainstorm of tears burst uncontrollably from each of them. Binu was forgotten, and they began to wail piteously.

General Deer bent low at the waist and cried at the riverbank as thoughts of another river took shape in his mind. The thatched hut he called home was on a river-bank. His father fished off the opposite bank, while his mother washed clothes on this side. And he cried and he cried, until he heard his sister calling his name from the hut. "The sweet potatoes are cooked. Go home and eat."

Chancellor Deer wept at some wild chrysanthemums and watched as they turned into speckled bamboo, out of which a turtledove flew. He chased after it, and ended up with a handful of wild chrysanthemum petals. Opening his hand, he cried out, "Turtledove, where is my Turtledove?"

Another boy wept at a tree and thought back to the time when he was apprenticed to a blacksmith. After his master had produced a hoe, a rake or a scythe, it was his responsibility to saw the proper length of wood and affix it as a handle. He had been well fed back then, but his belly wasn't as big as it was now.

The last deer-boy was the one with a gourd hanging from his neck, and he cried at their bound captive, who reminded him of his mother, then of his grandmother and his elder sister. As he cried, he called out, "Mother! Grandmother! Sister!" Binu, who was still gagged, did not respond, and the boy anxiously tore the gag from her mouth and cried out again, "Mum!"

Three of the boys suddenly recalled the road back home. One said he wanted to head east, home to his sweet potatoes. One said he wanted to go through Blue Cloud Pass, back to his mountain hut. The third said he wanted to go back to the Cotton City blacksmith to fix handles to hoes. Before the sun came up, they hurriedly left the forest. Only the boy with the gourd remained to watch over Binu. He was too young to recall the road home, so he removed the sash that covered her eyes, broke the chain with a rock, and said to her, "Get up, you can get up. You might as well go home too."

Binu's face, bathed in tears, was illuminated by the white light of suffering, which stung her eyes. She looked up at the limbs of the old elm tree and asked the boy, "What is on my face? Is it dew that has dropped from the tree?"

"What do you mean, dew?" he said. "Those are tears from your own eyes."

"What made you boys anger my tears like that? When tears flow from someone's eyes in Peach Village, that person's death is not far off. Child, your elder sister here is about to die!" She looked at the gourd hanging from his neck, and her eyes brightened, but only briefly. She reached out and pinched his cheek; he knocked her hand away. She stared at him, a sad smile appearing at the corners of her mouth. "It's you," she said. "No wonder you stayed behind with me. And no wonder you carry a gourd with you. Child, I've seen you in a dream. You will put me in the ground and you will cover my grave, for you are my gravedigger."

"What do you mean, cover your grave?" The boy was dumbstruck. "You are very much alive," he said. "How can I be your gravedigger? Do you want to be buried alive?"

"Death itself has sent you to be with me, child," said Binu. "It is here. Now that I've entered the forest, I shall never get to Great Swallow Mountain. And what good would come of it, even if I did, since my bundle is gone and my heart is broken. What can I give Qiliang if I do see him? You, child, are my gravedigger. Go to the tool shed and bring a shovel back with you. And a hoe."

Gravedigging

Dawn was on its way. Binu sat under the tree waiting for Death. The dark outlines of ancient trees were sketched against the blue sky, and a subtle, pungent odour of moss and vines spread through the air. The sky, fractured by random tree branches, sent light down to some spots, but kept others in dark seclusion. As she sat under the tree, Binu recalled again with resentment the prediction of the Kindling Village sorceresses. Why hadn't they told her that Death would come for her so soon, before she had even left Blue Cloud Prefecture, before she had even a glimpse of Great Swallow Mountain, and, worst of all, before she had a chance to see Qiliang? On her journey, she had heard warnings about wolf packs, poisonous snakes and bearded men, but not a word about children, terrifying children, half-human and half-deer. The children had awakened Binu's lachrymal glands by means of a demonic childish innocence. Her star had fallen. Every resident of Peach Village knew that when tears emerge from your eyes, those eyes will soon close for all eternity.

A herd of grey deer emerged from the shadows cast by the trees and circled the Deer King's grave. They studied the woman under the tree with a watchful eye. One of the deer, apparently the leader, came up and examined the broken chains, quickly discerning that they were not a weapon. It butted Binu gently with its horn. When it butted her a second time, it was clear that the deer regarded her as an intruder and wanted to drive her out of their territory.

Once she saw that this was a real deer, she said, "Deer, where would you have me go? Let me sit here for a little while. I won't be here for long before Death comes to claim me."

Dawn was about to break, and human sounds emerged from beyond the edge of the forest where the residents of Hundred Springs Terrace were getting out of bed, but Binu closed her eyes with exhaustion; it had become a habit to clutch her bundle to her before going to sleep, but now there was nothing to hold. She groped the ground around her with both hands and touched the loose chains lying beside her. She picked them up and heard the grass at the Deer King's gravesite swish back and forth, making her wonder if an unknown ghost was hidden in the grass. She dimly saw the wind blow up motes of dust, followed by puffs of blue smoke, as a child with horns on his head rose out of the grave. He had the limpid eyes and downy skin of a deer. He pointed to the gravesite and said to Binu, "Stop grumbling and come with me into my grave."

The only kindness Binu had been offered in the forest came from a graveside apparition. It frightened her enough to make her turn and run towards the deer shed, where the sound of boys skipping around the

102

forest had already started up. She wondered if the gourd boy had forgotten about getting the shovel and the hoe. He was her gravedigger, he would cover her grave, and she knew she had to find him. She ran as the first rays of morning sun reached her through the trees overhead, weeping into the hands that covered her face. A storm of tears sprang up on the forest floor, pools of water were left on the ground where the hem of her dress brushed past, and all the dead leaves and branches, all the withered ivy and wild mushrooms, were touched by the sorrow of the young woman from the south.

Soon she caught sight of her gravedigger, carrying a hoe and a spade over his shoulder as he walked through the forest in search of her. "It's almost light out," said the boy, handing her the hoe. "Why didn't you take advantage of the dark to die? Now that the sun's coming out, they'll all be up, and they'll see you, no matter where you dig."

Human footprints and deer hoofprints were visible all over the muddy ground; there were signs of digging next to a layer of fallen leaves. She stopped — she couldn't help herself — and began scraping at the ground with her hoe. She guessed what the deer-boys had buried there, and a sliver of hope, however illusory, rose in her: perhaps she could retrieve some of Qiliang's winter clothing, even a single sandal would do.

"I thought you said you wanted to die," the boy remarked. "So what are you doing, scraping the ground like that? I think you don't want to die at all, and you lied when you said you had to die because of a few tears. All along you wanted me to get you a hoe and a shovel so you could dig for your bundle."

"I wasn't lying. I would just like to see some of Qiliang's things before I die," Binu said. "I cannot accept the way things have turned out. I didn't lose sight of my bundle all the time I was on the road, avoiding bandits and highwaymen. But I couldn't avoid you boys."

"Don't blame us. We didn't ask you to come into our forest." Innocence shone in his eyes. "You're not going to find anything down there. The stuff in that bundle of yours is scattered all over the place. Each one of us hid what he took."

"Child, you could keep the sabre coins, I wouldn't mind. But you shouldn't have taken all of Qiliang's winter clothing. He's a grown adult, so his clothes will not even fit you."

"Who cares if they fit? We can sell them in the marketplace." The boy watched Binu for a while longer before running over and snatching the hoe out of her hands. "Use a tree branch if you want to dig for your bundle. You can't use my hoe. I know you lied to me, because everybody's afraid to die. What makes you different? Put anybody else in a grave, and all they want is to get out and run away. You're alive and well, so why would you want to dig your own grave? You're digging for your bundle, that's what you're doing."

Binu gazed sadly at the boy and sighed. "All right, I'll stop looking for my bundle. Let's go and find a spot facing the sun to dig a grave."

The boy threw the hoe and shovel on the ground and looked towards Hundred Springs Terrace. "What's this facing the sun business? What good will that do? Hear that? It's the horn sounding the morning hunt. Lord Hengming's horses will be out any minute now. Didn't you say I'm your gravedigger? Well, what's in it for me, now that your bundle is gone?"

"I was a gourd in my last life, child, and after I die I'll come back as one. You can pick it, take it home and cut it in half, and you'll have two ladles. If you don't want to do that, cut a hole in it and use it as a salt cellar. You can even make a lantern out of it."

"Who's interested in your ladles? Or your salt cellars?" The boy grunted with disdain, walked over, and felt inside the sleeves of Binu's robe. "But money can make the Devil turn a millstone. Do you have any sabre coins left?"

Binu patted her robe. "This is all you left me." Seeing the disappointment on his face, she reached up and removed a silver clip from her hair. "You take it. It won't do me any good now. However I comb my hair, Qiliang will never see it. You can give it to your wife someday."

"My wife? Do you think you can hire me for this little trinket? That sounds like a bad deal." He grumbled and pondered the situation for a while, but in the end he accepted Binu's hair clip, which he studied closely. "Is it real silver? This isn't a trick, is it?" Once he received Binu's sworn assurance, the boy smiled reluctantly, stuck the hair clip inside his ear and twisted it around, removing a glob of earwax. "Lord Hengming cleans his ears every day. The rich and the powerful like to do that, so from now on I'm going to use this to clean my ears, every single day!"

To make good his promise, he began fulfilling his duties as gravedigger. First, he fixed his gaze on an open spot beneath a pine tree, measured it, and, with some branches, outlined a rectangle big enough for someone lying down not quite flat. "After all," he said, "you'll be dead, with no need to cook or eat, so you won't need windows or doors; heat or cold won't be a concern, and you won't need a roof to keep out the elements. And you're small, so this will work fine."

Binu looked over the outlined gravesite and dimly spotted Death rising up from the rectangle, waiting eagerly for her. She was not afraid, but faced with the imminence of passing from life to death, of being buried in the forest with no one to raise a funeral banner and no one to shed a tear over her, her willingness to die became conditional. She decided that, before she died, she would have one last, tearful cry. So she walked around the rectangle and let her tears flow unchecked. They rained to the ground. Her long black hair, no longer bound by the clip, sobbed loudly in spite of its newly gained freedom, sending down a shower of tears.

"What are you doing?" cried the boy in alarm.

"I am encircling my grave, I am wailing at my grave. No one else will mark my death, so I must do it."

He stared at her in disbelief. "You women cannot leave well enough alone, alive or dead!"

106

When she had completed the ritual, she looked down at the gravesite through a veil of tears and thought about being interred beneath the pine tree. It was not near a road and did not face the sun, so it was not a good choice no matter how you looked at it. "Child," she said, offering one final suggestion, "could we not pick a brighter spot somewhere? I will return as a gourd, and this spot gets no sunlight. If, after I am under the ground, no gourd can grow, then what?"

"Sunlight? A gourd?" The boy shouted. "I knew all along that dying was the last thing you wanted. Well, you can be difficult if you want, but not with me playing Death."

"I am not being difficult. I'm just worried that, with so many deer in the area, if one of them were to eat the newly sprouted seed, there would be no gourd, and I wouldn't be reborn. Then I'd have died for nothing."

The boy flung his hoe at her feet, stood beside the spot for the hole, hands on his hips, and snorted angrily, "You're a liar! Dig your own grave and bury yourself! I'm not going to let you trick me any more."

They faced one another for a moment. The woman headed for death struggled to defend herself; the gravedigger was very angry. A tuft of brown feathers fell from the pine tree. The infuriated boy looked up and spotted a bird's nest in the treetop. The way it rose above the fork of the branches gave him an idea. "All right," he said, "I know a place, one where you'll never have to worry about not seeing the sun or about deer eating the vine. I'll tie you up, hang you from the tree, and let you die there." A cold, excited glare shone from his eyes. He picked up his hoe, went into the brush, and cut down some twigs. He selected one, rolled it up to test it and then let it snap back. "You said you want sunlight, right? Well, then, I'll tie you to the tree. Three of these ought to be enough for a skinny thing like you."

Binu looked up into the tree, where she saw the nest. "I am not a bird," she said, "and I'm not going up into a tree! Besides, even a bird falls to the ground when it dies. So does a leaf. How could you think of hanging me from a tree?"

"You're the one who said I'm your gravedigger," the boy complained. "I concern myself only with your death. And if I want you to die on a tree, then that is where you will die."

He stepped towards her, twig in hand, and was caught by surprise when she raised the hoe above her head. Though her face was bathed in tears, an unmistakeable resolve shone through. She would not die on a tree, she simply wouldn't. Even the boy could see that an emotionally overwrought woman who wanted to die was not about to yield on this point, and he found this amusing. "How can you be so stupid? After you're dead, you won't know anything, so why not just think of yourself as a tree branch? They all die on trees, don't they?"

"I am *not* a tree branch!" Binu replied angrily. "You cannot let me die up in a tree, child!"

The boy thought deeply and frowned. It was time for an ultimatum. "If not *in* the tree, then *under* the tree. This is your last chance. Does that sound all right to you? If not, then I'm leaving. I'll give you back your hair clip, and you can find someone else to dig your grave."

It was Binu's turn to compromise. She stepped towards the tree and studied the canopy of branches and leaves. "I suppose I'll have to do without sunlight. I shouldn't be so fussy, child, so don't be angry with me." She lifted up her skirt and squatted down in the grave plot, then tried lying down on her side. "It's big enough to allow me to be buried like this," she said eagerly. "You're a clever boy, and I'm lucky to have you to cover my grave. I am like your big sister, so who else would I get to do it?"

The forest floor was damp and loose, the sound of their digging muffled and soft. It should not have disturbed anyone outside the forest, and certainly no one in Hundred Springs Terrace. So when a retainer in a purple robe raced towards them, the boy was dumbfounded. "We've been spotted by Far-Seeing Eye," he shrieked in alarm. "Let's get out of here!" He threw down his hoe and took off running, only to be caught by the retainer almost as soon as he started.

Far-Seeing Eye, holding the boy in one hand and a flag in the other, walked menacingly up to Binu. "I had you in my sight last night as you prowled along the side of the moat. You must be an assassin."

Dangling from the crook of Far-Seeing Eye's arm, the boy said, "She's no assassin, she's a weeper."

"A weeper? I'd say she's a thief. You're right, she doesn't look like an assassin, so she must be a tree thief." Far-Seeing Eye said smugly, "I could tell there

109

was a tree thief from the other side of the moat just by the movement of leaves. So here I am, right again. You're here to steal a tree, aren't you?"

"I am no thief," said Binu, pointing to the hole in the ground. "We're digging not to steal a tree but to bury someone."

Obviously frightened of Far-Seeing Eye, the boy added, "I didn't choose to bury her. She hired me to dig a grave because she's tired of living."

Far-Seeing Eye released his grip on the boy and glared, first at him and then at Binu. The boy quickly shinnied up the tree and peered down at Far-Seeing Eye, a look of practised innocence on his young face. Binu, head lowered, kept her eyes fixed on the gravesite, a track of glistening tears on each cheek; both hands were shaking uncontrollably. Far-Seeing Eye kicked a clod of earth. "Who do you think you are, digging a grave here?" he thundered, as he stuck his flag into the ground. "Whose forest is this? Tell me that." He pointed to the golden panther on the flag. "You can die anywhere!" he shouted. "But you decided to pick this forest, one of Lord Hengming's treasured properties, a place of superb *feng shui* passed down from generation to generation. Not even we retainers are worthy of burial here, so how can a woman from who-knows-where expect it?"

Far-Seeing Eye's menacing words sent the boy higher up into the tree. "Where should she be buried, then?" he shouted, holding on to a branch.

With a glance at Binu, Far-Seeing Eye pointed to the northwest. "The potter's field. You people don't seem

110

to have eyes. Anonymous people who die in the streets are dragged off to be buried in the northwest potter's field."

Binu looked in the direction he was pointing. There at the far end of the forest was a patch of grey sky. It was the sky above the potter's field. She had seen that plot of wasteland on her way to Hundred Springs Terrace, weedy ground dotted with mushroom-shaped grave mounds. Crows filled the sky above. Where she was standing was a vast improvement over the potter's field; she stuck a tentative toe into the barely begun hole, then gazed pleadingly at Death. "Climb down out of that tree, child, and talk to this gentleman for me. All I want is this tiny spot of land. Why can't I have it?"

The boy rebuffed her from his perch in the tree, refusing to come down. "Why did you have to be so choosy? If you had let me do my job early on, you'd be in the ground now. Well, it's too late for regrets. Go and die in the potter's field."

Far-Seeing Eye pulled Binu up out of the hole, grabbed the hoe, and, before she could count to ten, the hole was filled in. He stuck the panther flag in the ground beside her and said, "Please don't get the idea that I am contemptuous of you. It's just that you should not have chosen Lord Hengming's forest for your gravesite. Don't be fooled by the way all those deer-boys are allowed to run and skip here in the forest. When they die, they are dragged off to be buried elsewhere. Even when we retainers fall ill and die, we are not buried here, so how can I allow you that privilege? Elder Sister, don't be stubborn, and don't try to pull any tricks on me. I am Far-Seeing Eye. Ask anyone and they will tell you who has the sharpest eyes of all of Lord Hengming's three hundred retainers. Even if you buried yourself thirty feet deep, you could not escape the power of my eyes; I'd come and dig you up."

Seeing that he was unmoving and overcome by exhaustion, Binu and the boy fell to the ground and slept.

The River Bend

The clang of the bell announcing a night hunt startled Binu awake. Sleeping near the river bend, she was once again dreaming of death; the bell brought the dream to an end. She awoke on her filled-in gravesite, and her first sight was a canopy of stars hanging low in the sky over the river bend, speaking to her of all the tiny details of death. To her it seemed the starry sky was stubbornly urging her to hold on to life. She was still alive, and that was a miracle, albeit a miracle she would not have chosen. Several watery pearls were frozen on her face, not dewdrops but tears she had shed as she dreamt. Why was she still alive after shedding all these tears? She recalled that her mother had told her that her father had shed a single tear over Lord Xintao, one teardrop on the mountain top, and was dead by the time he reached level ground. For three days now she had shed so many tears; this morning she had expected to be dead by nightfall and, as night was about to fall, she thought she would die before the sun rose again. She had anticipated her death for three days, only to open her eyes to a starry sky once more.

As she stood at the bend in the river, looking all around, she pinpointed the source of the sound of the bell — it came from the forest. Moonlight flooded the area, lending the water and the rank grass a cold gleam. The boy was sleeping next to her, but Binu could not waken her gravedigger; he must have been worn out by three days of waiting for her to die, waiting and digging, and doubting her motives.

By now, doubts had crept into Binu's mind as well. She could not say for sure if she was being untruthful or if she had been misled by the Peach Village *Rulebook for Daughters*. Perhaps her tears were worthless and she could shed them as much as she liked, without effect. Or perhaps her sadness did not count; her bitterness was a sham. Three days of waiting to die had taken its toll on her and yet she lived on, for which her Angel of Death had a bellyful of resentment.

"If you say you are going to die, then die," he had said.

She could tell that his patience had run out. As he slept on the ground, hoe in hand, snores of contempt emerged from his nostrils.

Binu failed again to waken him, so she went to look for a new gravesite. She found an ideal location, close to water, near the road, a pristine spot that descended from the riverbed; it was also far away from the frightful potter's field, but not far from Hundred Springs Terrace. The boy, finally awake, told her that the new territory near the bend in the river would one day become part of Hundred Springs Terrace. But that was in the future, and by then she would already be in the

114

ground and would have come back as a gourd. The people of Hundred Springs Terrace had yet to claim the marshy land by the river bend, so it was left to loaches, to reed blossoms, and to Binu. As dusk settled, a grand, canopied carriage drove by and stopped at the sight of Binu and the boy. Several men climbed down and, like stars attending the moon, guided an elderly official towards Binu. She assumed she was going to be driven away yet again, that this spot too was off limits.

Even before he had reached her, the official said, "What are you planting in this uncultivated spot, Elder Sister?"

"Gourds," she replied, not daring to reveal her true intent.

"Gourds are no good," the official said. "You should plant cotton. Aren't you aware that there is fighting going on in the west and in the south? If you plant cotton, you can use it to make uniforms for the warriors on the battlefields. Women, too, must make contributions to the state." The man's accent and diction were barely comprehensible to Binu, so after they had returned to the carriage and continued on their journey, she asked the boy if the man was Lord Hengming.

"Him? That was a royal emissary, sent by the King himself. Even Lord Hengming is afraid of him."

"I don't care where he came from," Binu replied, "I did not block his way, so he cannot stop me from digging a hole."

Torches in the forest turned half the sky red, the wind carried the voices of men, the cries of deer, and the whinnies of horses to the river bend. Binu did not know what was happening in Hundred Springs Terrace. She nudged the boy, who jumped to his feet, and when he heard the call of deer whistles he exclaimed, "A hunt!"

He gazed longingly over at the forest beyond the river, and said, "It's a night hunt, a night hunt! I've never been on one of those. Forget about the grave, I'm going back to being a deer-boy."

"You can't leave," said Binu. "When I say I'm going to die, I'm going to die. Who knows, I might be dead when the sun comes up. If you leave, who will throw dirt into my grave?"

A look of loathing came over the boy's face. He glared at Binu for a moment, then abruptly scooped out a hoefull of dirt and flung it at her. "Throw dirt! Throw dirt! I'll throw it for you right now. It's not fair; always saying you're going to die, but never actually doing it. You've held me up long enough, and all for a measly ear-pick."

"I understand your feelings, and it confounds me too that I am still alive. Living is hard, but dying is harder." Binu looked up into the sky above the river bend. "A while ago I asked the stars what kept me from dying. I dreamed I was dead, the same dream I've had many times, but I awoke, and there again was the starry sky."

"You're lazy, just sitting around waiting to die. You won't hang from a tree, because a hanged ghost has a long tongue, and you find that ugly. You won't jump into the river because a drowned ghost will float off in

116

the water. Instead you insist on being buried in the ground. What's so good about that anyway?"

"I am a gourd, child. How can I come back as a gourd if I'm not in the ground?"

This infuriated the boy. "You are not a gourd. You are a dung beetle. Only dung beetles burrow into the ground to die."

The boy ran off into the night, leaping nimbly over the hoe and disappearing from sight in the direction of the hunt. Binu could not hold him back, and again she stood alone, this time in the chill of moonbeams. She hadn't known that life could contain so much suffering, that even dying could be such hard work. Winds rustled the reeds on the riverbank and swept at her hair. She looked down at the ground, where she saw her own shadow. Ghosts do not cast shadows, and she definitely had one. After three days and three nights, how could she still be dragging a shadow up and down the river bend? She thought back to the ways of dying that the boy had mentioned. Hanging from a tree was the quickest and easiest. She could do that without help; all she needed was a sash. But the boy was right, she'd seen people who had died that way, with their eyes popping and their tongues hanging out, and the scene had terrified her.

The second way lay right in front of her. All she had to was walk up to the deepest part of the river and drown herself. That wouldn't be difficult either. Just lie down and let the water swallow her up. But she was a gourd, not a fish. Gourds need to sprout, and if there was no earth from which the shoot could emerge, there would be no gourd and she would have no rebirth. The cold ripples of the moonlit water filled her with terror. With water there would be no rebirth, and more than twenty years of bitterness would have been endured in vain, all those tears shed for nothing. More than twenty years of days and nights, each passed in futility.

Binu stuck one foot into the water, while the other leg held itself back. A stalemate raged for a while, until she decisively pulled the first foot back onto dry land. Death by water was out of the question, no matter how easy it might seem. She consoled her wet foot, and herself as well, that she would die sooner or later, but it would be on solid ground.

Silence reigned on her side of the river, but from somewhere in the distance came the croak of a frog, then another. It must be my frog, she thought, somewhere in the grass over there. She searched the riverbank for a few moments, then suspected that the croaking may well have come from the roadside. "This is no time for hide-and-seek," she muttered. "I'm not interested in you, so go and look for your son." She had abandoned all thoughts of finding the frog, since they had parted company and were no longer travelling companions. If it had been a person, that would have been wonderful, for then she wouldn't have to travel alone. But they were women existing in two different worlds and speaking of different matters. The living woman was searching for her husband, the dead woman for her son. They might travel together, but would never *be* together.

So Binu decided to return to her gravesite; in the moonlight it had the look of an unfinished grave, but also a crude and simple home. It was warmer inside than outside, for there was no wind down there. She was on the verge of sliding into the hole when, suddenly, she spotted the frog — it was crouching in her grave, looking up to hear what she had to say. In the days since she had last seen the frog, it had grown wizened and its blind eyes were far more sorrowful, emitting a light of hopelessness.

"Get out! Go and search for your son," cried Binu as she knelt beside the hole. "Come out of there. My good feelings for you are gone. I prepared a bundle for Qiliang and let you hide inside. Now I've worked hard to dig a grave, only to have you come and take it over. A frog you may be, but you have taken advantage of me. A little thing like you has no business in a hole this big. There is mud on the riverbank, and any spot will do for you. Why have you chosen my hole?"

The frog refused to come out, apparently having decided to end its journey of misery in this hole in the ground. Binu did not know if it planned to occupy the hole alone or was prepared for them to die together. Whatever its motives, she would have none of it. She clapped her hands and stamped her feet, but the frog was unmoved. Finding it impossible to get rid of the frog, Binu grew wilful. She picked up the hoe and brandished it in front of the hole.

"If you don't come out of there," she vowed, "I'll come down, and we'll see who is left standing. Even if this was just a dry well, it would still be reserved for me alone."

The frog stayed put, a single tear on its face bringing a white light into the darkness. Binu turned away to avoid looking at that tear. Sorrow had lost its power on this night; a woman who did not cry had already shed all the tears she had, and the tears of the frog were now someone else's burden. Neither could get a reaction from the other. So a long confrontation between a pair of one-time travelling companions developed at the river bend, and an air of antagonism turned the atmosphere icy. Even the water flowing in the moonlight gasped tensely.

Back at Hundred Springs Terrace, Lord Hengming had chosen to ride each of his precious Snow Mountain horses instead of a horse-man.

Tens of thousands of thoroughbred Blue Cloud white horses had galloped off with generals and their troops to battlefields during three years of war, and even before the winds of war in the southwestern border region had abated, all the remaining horses — fine steeds, sick ponies and old nags — had followed the wall builders north. All three hundred of Lord Hengming's retainers knew how passionate their master was about his hunting outings, that he would rather die than give them up; when he saw how his stable was being depleted of horses, he grew sallow, and the sharp eyes of his retainers spotted that his idle buttocks had grown even more sallow than his face. He had received a special dispensation, given only to nobility, to keep three of his favourite horses, but the retainers, who were accustomed to doing everything necessary to lessen their master's worries and ease his hardships, sought replacements for the missing horses. By pooling their wisdom and efforts, a fervent tide of creativity and thinking swept through Hundred Springs Terrace, leading eventually to the invention of horse-men.

This invention created a glorious new page in the *Old Chronicle of Archery*. Hundred Springs Terrace's horsemen opened up a new world, and not just in Blue Cloud Prefecture; the rulers and aristocrats of seven prefectures and eight counties followed its example, and this enterprising practice for the greater good of the Kingdom was praised by the Court, with the King announcing considerately that the horse-men were to be exempt from military conscription. As the news spread, young men in cities and rural areas everywhere began to vie for this new occupation, producing a craze for running with heavy loads. They ran up mountains with boulders on their backs; they ran through forests with logs on their backs; they ran at home carrying their aged and unproductive grandparents on their backs. They practised equine gaits, breathing and snorting characteristics, even whinnying, as they ran like horses, only faster.

Riding humans for the hunts became fashionable in aristocratic circles, gaining steadily in popularity. But, as with the development of anything new, problems soon arose. Arrows flew in the forests and on mountain slopes, driving great quantities of wild deer, muntjacs, rabbits and mountain gazelles out of the hills and up to

121

the mountaintops, while birds flew off to unknown places; soon the joys of hunting were under serious threat. Horse-men had bows but no targets, they had speed but nothing to chase. With the disappearance of quarry, they could only return empty-handed.

Seeing a permanent scowl on the face of Lord Hengming, the Hundred Springs Terrace retainers embarked upon a new and vigorous campaign of exploration and invention. One of them discovered in the Bluegrass Ravine People Market a skinny, undernourished boy who ran around while other boys up in trees threw woven darts at him. The darts had the boy running and skipping, just like a deer. The retainer's eyes flashed at first sight, and he bought the boy on the spot. On the way back to Hundred Springs Terrace, the boy followed along behind, timidly asking what lay ahead for him. "Your Lordship, have you bought me to make me a horse-man? Would you like to climb up on my back and try me out?"

The retainer replied frankly, "You, a horse-man? Why, you haven't even grown hair down between your legs. You will not be a horse-man, you'll be a deer-boy."

Down came the drawbridge, and there sat Lord Hengming, perched on top of his favourite Snow Mountain horse, River-and-Mountains. The horse raised its massive head and sent an intimidating whinny in the direction of the horse-men. Treasure and Beauty, the other two horses saved by the dispensation, were being led by grooms, their manes waving proudly in the wind, their shoes glistening; their big, beautiful eyes, fixed on the horse-men, were filled with the

122

contemptuous look of the genuine article eyeing up an imposter.

The horse-men were immediately made aware of their debased status. They had been looking forward to running riderless like wild horses but, as soon as the drawbridge came down, they discovered that, with no riders on their backs, and no daylight to guide them, they could no longer run like regular horses, let alone wild ones. They were disconcerted by the absence of weight; and though they ran at an acceptable speed and whinnied like real horses, even the greatest among them ran awkwardly and with no confidence.

A retainer shouted to them, "Wild horses, is that what you think you are? You are nothing but brainless creatures running blindly!"

Lord Hengming armed his bow, but the fake running style of the horse-men, neither like men nor like horses, stopped him from firing an arrow. He shouted angrily, "What contemptible creatures! They have forgotten how to run without riders on their backs. Bring on the deer-boys. Instead of horses, I'll hunt deer!"

The deer-boys, waiting quietly in the forest, whooped with delight. For what was probably the first time, they could stand with pride in the presence of horse-men. They fixed their horns on their heads, attached their deer tails, and began leaping past the horse-men, basking in new-found glory.

Figures flashed in the torch-lit forest. The poor deer-boys, enjoying the sense of pride in having a master for once, romped happily in their forest, frolicked like creatures swept up in a life-changing euphoria, gambolled as gratitude overflowed in their hearts. Some bounded like grey deer, some like whitetails, and some like sikas. Two courageous brothers actually sprang right in front of Lord Hengming, taunting him to chase after them. This intense provocation elicited an excited cry from Lord Hengming — "Excellent!" — as his cypress arrows whizzed among the trees of the forest, his quiver quickly emptied. River-and-Mountains was soon tired out from the maniacal running about, as Lord Hengming immediately realized when his hand touched the horse's sweaty back. "River-and-Mountains is worn out. Change horses!"

The horse-men, who were sitting dispiritedly on the ground, jumped to their feet. One of their number, fleet-footed, kind-hearted Moon Rider, invigorated by the shout, galloped up to Lord Hengming, bent down, and said, "It has been many days since you last rode me, Your Lordship. Please, up onto my back."

"Are you a Snow Mountain thoroughbred? No, you are only a horse-man." Lord Hengming drove the hapless Moon Rider away with his whip. "Didn't I say that I will not ride you horse-men tonight?"

A groom led Treasure up and gave Lord Hengming a hoist up. To fill time while someone went back to fetch more arrows, the retainers scoured the forest with their torches to measure how the night hunt had gone so far, taking a red seal with them. They picked up each deer-boy who had been hit by an arrow and examined him, starting from his hindquarters. They stamped a panther insignia next to each arrow that had found its mark. Most of the boys had been hit in the rump, to the boisterous delight of the retainers. Knowing the merciful nature of their master, how he hated to take the lives of his subjects, he had catered for the boys' safety by using only cypress arrows and honing his archery skills to perfection. He considered the rump to be the only appropriate target; all others were misses. When the retainers were affixing insignias, disagreements often arose. "That's not his thigh. His rump is just too small. This counts as part of his rump, so it's a hit!"

The retainers who had run back to fetch more arrows returned with disturbing news: there were no more cypress arrows, only metal ones. They held up several quivers, which clinked as the arrows inside shifted. "Why are you bringing those to me?" Lord Hengming demanded. "Do you expect me to shoot metal arrows at children?"

"We thought you were enjoying yourself, Your Lordship, and did not want your pleasure to come to an end. It was just a precaution."

"My pleasure has not come to an end," Lord Hengming barked. "I have only ridden one of my Snow Mountain horses. How could I already be out of arrows? Who ordered the arrows for me? Why are there so few made of cypress? Stop treating me like a child."

None of the retainers dared offer a response, provoking their master further. "What are you gawking at? Why are you all standing around looking stupid? Go and bring back all the arrows that were shot."

By this time, the deer-boys were beginning to get restless, wanting to display both gratitude for Lord Hengming's show of mercy and their willingness to do his bidding, and also to show the failed horse-men that they were the stars tonight. Without warning, they begged Lord Hengming in disorderly but moving voices, "Use real arrows, we're not afraid. Only cowards are afraid of real arrows. Good Master, we deer-boys are here to serve you!"

Lord Hengming, deeply touched by the deer-boys' expression of loyalty, reached out for the new quiver and raised it as an expression of kindness. Struggling to control his emotions, he said, "Good! Wonderful! Marvellous! Inscribe these children's brave words on your bamboo tallies."

Quickly ordering someone to open a bamboo tablet, the retainer replied, "Yes, Your Lordship. I will put it all down: Your Lordship's loving kindness towards the people, and their gratitude and loyalty towards Your Lordship. I will record it all in a volume and place it in a chest in the Eastern Pavilion, for someday it will come in handy."

A silence fell over the forest, abruptly broken by a fearful shout from another of the retainers: "They're fighting! The horse-men and deer-boys are fighting!"

Lord Hengming was shocked by the horse-men's appalling behaviour. The tauntings of the deer-boys had led to a collective loss of control. Older and stronger, and shielded by the darkness of the night, the horse-men began by attacking the deer-boys' leaders, though they quickly moved on to tracking down the other deerboys, angrily beating and kicking them when they caught them. In all the years Lord Hengming had held his hunts, the horse-men and deer-boys had always been on their best behaviour, walking the paths they were given, and he was traumatized by the breakdown in discipline that he was witnessing. But rage soon replaced trauma.

"Shoot them!" he ordered, his face scarlet with anger. He commanded his retainers to raise their bows and shoot metal arrows. "If you kill them, I'll take the blame!"

A storm of arrows flew into the forest, from which emerged terrified shrieks and the sound of panicky running. The rhythm of death played out by the rainstorm of arrows spurred the targeted creatures into a cadence of madness as they ran for their lives. In the torchlight, the herd of deer-boys looked like fleeing deer; the horse-men were transformed into galloping wild horses. One by one, the torches in the forest were extinguished, and the sound of the hunt dropped mysteriously into the river and sank to the bottom.

There was a sound of intermittent creaks of carriage wheels on the road, and a hearse pulled by a pair of oxen appeared on the road. Binu spotted someone familiar among all the moving figures: it was Wuzhang again, sitting in the driver's seat, bent over at the waist and holding the reins with his feet; standing behind him was the boy, her gravedigger, returned from the hunt and looking triumphant. He waved to Binu, an arrow in his hand, announcing nightmarish news:

"Don't die now," he said. "Get up out of that hole. I sold you. You are now the widow of a thief named Qinsu!"

At first, Binu could not understand what he was saying. She approached him. "Who sold whom?" But as she drew near to the oxcart and saw the black coffin, the realization hit her: no one would bring her a coffin out of the goodness of his heart. This was someone else's coffin! She stepped back to get a good look at the boy, suddenly noticing his new attire: a white funeral robe. Before she could ask where he had got it from, several ferocious men jumped down off the cart and rushed at her like wild beasts. Now she understood: someone else had died and she had been sold. The boy had sold her to a dead man!

Like hawks swooping down on small birds, the Hundred Springs Terrace retainers easily caught Binu and carried her over to the cart, where she was tied up with ropes again. At first she struggled, but not for long, as water spilled from her body. They watched her look up into the sky, murmuring a single phrase over and over again: "I should have gone down, I should have gone down."

"What is she muttering?" the retainers asked the boy. "Gone down where?"

The boy pointed to the hole by the river bend. "Into the ground. She regrets not going into the ground when she had the chance."

"If she had," one of the retainers said, "we'd just have had to dig her up. Dead, she goes into a coffin.

Living, she accompanies the coffin of the retainer Qinsu with her wails. She can't get away, dead or alive."

One of the other retainers was puzzled by all the water splashing on his robe. "This woman must have been in the water," he shouted. "She's drenched."

"Be careful," the boy said, "that isn't water, those are her tears. She is a weeper!"

The retainers laughed. "A weeper, you say? Then she is well-chosen. What could be better than a weeper wailing for a dead man?"

As they flicked the strange water from their hands, they hurriedly dressed her in a white funeral robe and placed a white three-sided cap on her unruly hair, finishing off with a white sash around her waist. Then they stood back to admire her in her fitted funeral clothes. The look of sorrow on her face was just right for a new widow. When they had finished with her, one of them nailed an iron ring into the side of the coffin, while another fastened a chain around Binu's ankle, which was then attached to the ring. With a clang, Binu was chained to the coffin, and the oxcart set off along the road.

Fragrant Forest Station

The nearer they came to Pingyang Prefecture, the farther they were from the mountains, which rolled on into the distance like waves until they dissolved into a hazy skyline. The seemingly boundless plain was a blanket of green and yellow, the colours of abundance. After passing fields of oats, there were increasing numbers of small communities of thatched huts, with village dogs and chickens running around in the open, but few people. Clusters of purple knotweed grew at the side of ditches, looking like flower beds from a distance. The plain was flat and open, under a sky that seemed to go on forever, while the sun seemed lower, like a fireball baking the farmhouses in the middle of the golden yellow oat fields.

The boundless plain made Binu lightheaded, and she lost all sense of direction. But what did that matter, since she was still chained to Qinsu's coffin? They told her that Seven-Li Cave, the birthplace of Qinsu, was to the north, on the way to Great Swallow Mountain.

"After we cross this plain," the driver said, "we'll see mountains. Those are the northern mountains. When you see them, Great Swallow Mountain will be in sight and when you see Great Swallow Mountain, you'll be able to see your man. You hitched a ride on the right cart this time, so no more suicide attempts. Be content with your lot."

Binu watched the boy's filthy face swaying on top of the coffin. He was no longer her gravedigger, no longer in the service of the Angel of Death. Instead he had taken on the loathsome mission of chaining her to a coffin and keeping her alive. He now had a firm grasp on the tail that was her life. She'd lost even the right to die when Hundred Springs Terrace married her off to a corpse. Hundred Springs Terrace was heaven on earth for so many people, but had become hell on earth for Binu. They had stolen her bundle, stolen her body, and finally stolen even her sorrow, her tears, and her right to die.

Binu looked down at the iron ring attached to the coffin, a great big hand that held her tightly and never loosened its grip. It was the man's hand, the hand of a corpse, holding on to her, repeating a sorrowful command, filled with vanity, "Cry, oh cry, cry for me, cry louder!"

Binu related her tearful complaint to every person she met along the way, even to roadside chickens, ducks, pigs and sheep. "I am from Peach Village, the wife of Wan Qiliang." Her laments were interpreted by people as mourning for the dead. Throughout the trip, she wailed, crying for herself and for Qiliang. No sounds emerged, only tears, which flowed drop by drop in a stream in her wake, dampening the roadside. All the bright-eyed people who passed by the hearse regarded her as a grieving widow, not noticing the chain that was visible only beneath her white robe, choosing instead to comment animatedly on the panther flag and the cypress coffin, with its subtle fragrance. How they envied the man lying inside.

"How splendid to be a retainer in Hundred Springs Terrace," they said, "even when you're dead. They sleep in fine coffins and are accompanied by virtuous wives and filial sons. Ah, such good fortune!"

They had locked her up at the entrance to the cave of death, where, if you stood up, you lived, but if you jumped down, you died. Binu, however, could neither stand up nor jump down. She was forced to lean up against the coffin of a man she did not know and travel north, feeling that she was not a woman on an oxcart, but a gourd that was being taken northwards on an alien road, as if carried along by ocean waves.

"Is it still death that you seek? Do you want to go to Great Swallow Mountain, or not?"

Repeated provocations by the driver and the boy had worn her out. They could not know that she had forsaken both life *and* death. In the mornings, the sun warmed her robe with a promise of life; but at night, the cart was swamped in darkness, and a chill spread across the coffin. The north became for her a curtain of black, and the road to Great Swallow Mountain seemed longer even than her own life.

The boy kept coming over to tug her hair. "Let's hear you breathe," he said. "Stop pretending you're dead. Let's see you move. Say something."

Binu shoved his hand away.

132

"Is that all you can do?" he demanded. "You don't speak, you don't eat, you don't even pee. How am I supposed to know you're alive? At most you're half-dead."

Binu looked down at the once-dry grass at the side of the road, which now glistened with crystal-like tear-drops.

"Child," she said, pointing at the damp grass, "I am still crying, and that proves that I am alive."

They neared Fragrant Forest Station before nightfall.

A pair of grotesque young men came running out before the cart reached the station, their faces painted with anti-curse markings, their nostrils stuffed with grey-green mugwort, their hands wrapped in treated rags, for the plague had arrived already. They stood in the road to stop the cart and declared that coffins with corpses were forbidden from entering the station.

Since they were now in Pingyang Prefecture, Lord Hengming's travel permit was of no use, so Wuzhang complained to the men, "This is no ordinary coffin. You can see for yourselves there's a living person chained to it. What do we do about her if we cannot take the coffin in?"

The men walked up and saw that Binu's ankle was in fact chained to the coffin. "What's this all about?" they exclaimed. "Do all Blue Cloud Prefecture coffins come equipped with iron rings, so you can chain the dead man's wives to them?"

"No," replied Wuzhang, "only this one, and this is the only woman chained to one."

The men from the station suggested that Wuzhang unchain her. A long hesitation followed, before he turned to Binu and said, "If you swear an oath that you won't try to run away or kill yourself, I'll unlock the chain."

With an indifferent look, she replied, "What sort of oath do you want, Elder Brother? Why would anyone who is not afraid to die worry about an oath?"

"I know you're not afraid to die," he said. "But you are still concerned that your husband might freeze to death on Great Swallow Mountain, so swear on the life of your husband, Qiliang."

Binu shook her head. "Unchain me or not, it's up to you, but I will not swear on the life of Qiliang."

The men were confused.

"She's half-dead anyway, so let's all pitch in and unload her along with the coffin," said Wuzhang.

It was a time-consuming affair, and night had fallen by the time Qinsu's coffin was lying in a field of oats, the chained Binu bent over it. The oat field reached out its slender fingers to stroke the black lacquered coffin and Binu's white robe, perhaps because the oat field had never received such exceptional visitors. Driven by curiosity, the oats took a coffin and a living woman generously to their bosom. In her white robe, she was like a cotton cloud settling over the field.

"Go and watch over her," Wuzhang ordered the boy.

The boy bounded away from the driver. "I'm not going to sleep in the open air," he said. "I want to sleep in Fragrant Forest Station. Besides, I have to feed and water the oxen."

"Not today. I'll do it." Wuzhang ran after the boy. "Don't throw my kindness to the wind. Stay with her tonight, and I'll make it up to you with a big chunk of flatbread tomorrow in Seven-Li Cave."

The boy ran up to Binu, grabbed her arm and raised it, to force her to swear an oath to the driver. "Swear it!" he yelled, giving her a shove. "How hard can that be? All you have to do is swear, and you won't be chained to a coffin like a dog any more. Do that and we can all go into the station."

Binu swayed under the assault of the boy's violent shoves. "Stop that," she said. "I'd like to do what you want, and I don't want to cause trouble, but I cannot risk Qiliang's life in an oath."

"If you're not thinking of dying and you aren't going to run away, what's the problem? Since you won't swear it, I'll do it for you: If I try to kill myself or run away, then let my husband Qiliang freeze to death in the snow or be crushed by rocks from the mountain!"

Binu shuddered and reached out to cover his mouth, but was too late. He ran out of the oat field and looked back to see her kneeling on the ground, her face bathed in tears.

"All right," she said, "you win. Now that you've sworn on the name of Qiliang, I will not try to kill myself and I will not run away."

That night in Fragrant Forest Station, Binu sat in an oat field in the company of a coffin.

When the dim candlelight from the station went out, total darkness enveloped her. Winds blew across the field, and the black coffin was swallowed up in the darkness, except for the gold inlays, which gave off a forbidding glare. At first she put as much distance between her and the coffin as she could, but after a while, either to seek shelter from the wind or for companionship, she slowly returned to it and so passed the night in yet another alien place. Terror that could not be overcome was now a part of the night. She was in the company of a dead man; he was her companion. Binu kept her eyes wide open, awaiting the arrival of the harvesting ghosts. She saw the hand of the wind as it invaded the oat field, which turned sideways to get away. She watched the moon's hand stroke the oat field, the tips of the stalks giving out a sharp, silvery light. But she saw no scythe-wielding ghosts.

From Peach Village all the way to this plain in a foreign land, no one had been willing to listen to Binu, so she was prepared even to have a conversation with ghosts. But they did not come, and so she still had no one to talk to. She knocked on the coffin:

"Big Brother, Big Brother, is your name Qinsu?" she asked. "Qinsu, Qinsu, you were a thief, but I'm not afraid. I don't have anything worth stealing. You are dead, and I'm still not afraid, because I've already died several times. I just need to ask you something: with all the women in the world you could have chained to your coffin, why did you choose me?" The wind stopped while she was talking, and the oat stalks quit rustling. "Speak, speak, speak." She had no more to say. Now that she had said all she wanted to say, her tears flowed unchecked onto the coffin and slid down the four sides; the big black coffin was bathed in a shower of tears. At first it did not move, but gradually sounds of distress emerged from it, and Binu could feel it tremble under her hand. She could not keep it from moving. The wind got up, stirring the oat stalks so that they battered against the coffin. Binu heard the muffled sound of a man crying deep inside. It was Qinsu's ghost. The sound carried feelings of remorse and obstinacy, as it released a steady, sorrowful refrain to Binu: "Seven-Li Cave, Seven-Li Cave, Seven-Li Cave!"

They were going to Seven-Li Cave, Qinsu's birthplace. She was powerless to argue with a ghost. "I have come from Peach Village. I am the wife of Wan Qiliang."

She had told so many people about her background, but the living ignored her, and now so did a ghost. The voice in the coffin was both sorrowful and determined, "Seven-Li Cave, Seven-Li Cave, Seven-Li Cave!"

"I am not going to Seven-Li Cave, I am from Peach Village. I am the wife of Wan Qiliang," she shouted at the coffin. This had no effect the first time, so she shouted it over and over again, and the human voice finally overcame that of the ghost. She listened as the sound from inside the coffin began to sink, until it was no more than a thin sigh. The coffin stopped moving, and she sat down.

Cold late-autumn winds began to blow from the wildwoods. The night before, Binu had looked forward to dying; the night before, the chilled wind had been her Angel of Death. But this night was different. An oath uttered by the boy had changed everything. She could no longer look forward to dying; she had to live on for the sake of Qiliang. She covered herself with a blanket of fallen oat stalks, and the chilled winds stopped. For the first time in days, Binu felt hungry, so she picked several oats and put them in her mouth. As she chewed them she kept an eye on the coffin, but her eyelids got heavier and heavier and sleep was on its way. She was immediately visited by a dream in which the legendary ghostly harvesters, none of them familiar to her and all carrying scythes, floated up in the night. They were wearing Qiliang's headdress and his coat, tied with his jade-inlaid belt. The sound of harvesting rose from the earth as all the harvesting ghosts turned into likenesses of Qiliang. She imagined that he was one of them, but even after she had shouted herself hoarse, the ghosts kept their silence. In the dream Binu wept, and the ghosts stopped what they were doing. One of them led the way to her, carrying a bundle of oat stalks.

"I am not Qiliang," it said, "so don't cry. Here, these oats are for you."

All the other ghosts threw bundles of oats at her feet. "Qiliang is not here," they said, "so don't cry, don't cry; these oats are for you."

The next morning, the carter and the boy picked Binu up out of stacked bundles of oat stalks.

"I've never seen ghosts treat anyone this well in my life. Woman, you are pitied only by ghosts. Just look how many oat stalks they cut down for you!"

Standing in the morning sun in an oat field, a bundle of fresh oats in her arms, and amid the gleeful shouts of a boy, Binu looked down at Qinsu's coffin and saw that

138

it was framed by the fruits of a fine harvest. The night was over, and the coffin lid was covered by newly harvested oats on which translucent, crystalline dewdrops rested.

Seven-Li Cave

The hearse kept moving eastward, meandering its way out of the mist, passing a graveyard and a grove of trees before finding a village hidden beneath the ground. Swirls of kitchen smoke rose slowly from many caves, through whose openings children's heads could be seen from time to time. Incense smoke rose from a giant cave, from which emerged the sounds of people chanting and praying.

"We've arrived at Qinsu's home," the carter said to his two passengers. "Bang on the coffin and wail. And hurry up."

Knocking on the coffin, the boy looked at Binu and said, "She's not wailing, and she's the virtuous wife. A filial son isn't supposed to cry before the virtuous wife, is he?"

Wuzhang glared at Binu, and from the indifferent look on her haggard face he knew that, even though her tears might be as free-flowing as the ocean, whether or not she made any noise was up to her. Her ankle chain had been removed, because he was confident he could control her feet. Her tears and sadness, on the other hand, were beyond his reach. So he shifted his focus from the virtuous wife to the filial son, and his demeanour. The broad smile on the boy's face showed that this was all a game to him. With a mixture of anger and anxiety, the carter picked up his whip with his feet and raised a red welt on the boy's face. The painful howls drew heads out from the caves, sallow faces materializing in the smoky mist.

The women and children timidly and curiously gazed at the oxcart from the protection of their caves, leaving it to the men to come out to greet the newcomers. Clutching stalks of wheat in their hands, they glared at the people on the cart until an old man broke the silence by telling them that their unannounced visit had ruined an auspicious day. The wails had interfered with the chanting of the wheat sutra, and that could augur badly for next year's wheat harvest, and beyond.

"We don't care about wheat," said Wuzhang. "We're delivering Qinsu's coffin. Ask his family to come and claim it."

No one stepped up. There was no interest in a woman and a boy in mourning garb. The luxurious coffin, on the other hand, aroused the curiosity of a few of the men. One old fellow came up and touched the black lacquer surface, even gouging out some gold powder and holding it up to the sun.

Another one, a pock-marked man, banged on the side of the coffin and bent his head to listen. "This must be a wooden rice bin," he said. "But why is there someone sleeping inside?"

"It's not a rice bin," shouted the disgruntled carter, "it's a coffin. And that's Qinsu sleeping in it. You remember Qinsu, don't you? Well, here are his virtuous wife and filial son, who have escorted the coffin home. Where is the family? Which one of you is his mother? Come up here."

Several old women clad in palm bark crawled out of the cave to watch. Bent over at the waist, their legs bare, they looked like scarecrows.

"Whose son is Qinsu?"

There was no response from the women; clearly none of them was his mother.

Giving up on them, the carter shouted to the men, "Come and take a look at Qinsu's hands."

Signalling the boy to open the coffin, he said, "See, this is Qinsu of Seven-Li Cave. You may not recall his name, but you ought to recognize those hands."

An old man with a wise face elbowed his way up and stared curiously at the writing on the dead man's wrists. He asked the boy, "Is that a drawing of a horse or a fish on his hand?"

The boy laughed. "A horse or a fish, you say? They're words."

"I know that," the old man said. "I want to know what they mean."

"You don't even recognize these two words? The one on the left means robber, and the one on the right means thief."

One by one, the people circling the coffin backed away.

142

"What? He's a robber and a thief?" The wise old man, the first among them to grasp the significance, was so outraged that his face reddened and his white goatee quivered. He grabbed hold of the carter's belt. "How dare you send the coffin of a robber and a thief to Seven-Li Cave! This place is famous for its poverty, but no man in our lineage has ever been a thief, and no woman has ever been a prostitute. No robber or thief comes from here."

Wuzhang hurriedly brushed the white silk covering from the dead man's face with his elbow. "Is Qinsu's family all dead?" He jumped onto the cart and yelled, "Has his mother died? If his parents are dead, how about his siblings? They can't all be dead too? If they are, there must be other relatives. Why doesn't someone come forward to claim him? This is Qinsu, from Seven-Li Cave. Take a good look at his face. Someone help me out here and take the coffin away."

A limping man in a coat of hemp cloth was leering at Binu. He walked up to the carter, who said, "Are you Qinsu's brother? Or maybe his cousin? Come and take the coffin off my hands."

"I don't want that coffin. I'd have to get help to bury it. But I'd be happy to take the living off your hands." He nudged the carter. "I could take the widow for a wife, and the boy as my son."

"I assumed you were all not quite right in the head," said Wuzhang, grimacing in anger as he realized the man's intentions. "That shows how much I know. You're smarter than I figured. No dead man for you, but you'd be willing to take on a wife and a son, all for free. Well, keep dreaming."

By now most of the villagers had gathered round a few of the older, wiser men, talking things over as they sized up the hearse from a distance. Some stared at the people, while others focused on the two Blue Cloud oxen; some, who were more concerned with the coffin's capacity, ran over to measure its length and height. "Three loads of wheat flour, no problem," they said.

They solemnly announced their decision: "The coffin will stay in Seven-Li Cave to store grain to keep it from rotting. As for Qinsu's wife and son, they can stay or leave; it's up to them. But the dead man, Qinsu, is unwelcome here. You can take him away and bury him wherever you please. Seven-Li Cave may be a poor place, but rites and morality are important here. There is no place for a robber and a thief, whether he is from the area or not, and no matter where he's been, even if he has returned from serving the King. Seven-Li Cave will not stand by and allow such a man to be buried here."

The irate carter could not control his tongue. He smirked. "What kind of place is this? You're poor and lowly, and yet you talk about honour. You can forget about the rest if you won't take the dead man. All I can leave you is a few wheel ruts."

It had taken a great deal of trouble to get to Seven-Li Cave, but it took none to leave. The carter flicked his whip, and the dead man, the living, the oxen, and the coffin were on the road again. They never expected that their trip to Seven-Li Cave would end in such haste,

144

and the carter could not stop cursing, furious that the villagers had drifted back into the incense cave even before the cart had left. "They can't read a word, but they know how to recite chants! They won't claim a member of their own family, and all they care about is a bumper wheat crop! I hope they have a flood next year, then a drought and, after that, locusts. Then we'll see what kind of harvest they have!"

Binu turned to gaze at Seven-Li Cave in the smoky mist, the look in her eyes turning to bewilderment. This was the first time since leaving Peach Village that she had actually tasted the sorrow of others; it was bitter and it was cold. Qinsu's spirit began to rage uncontrollably. Filled with remorse and guilt, she patted the coffin to comfort the corpse inside. "Qinsu, don't be sad. It's not that your family didn't want you or your coffin, just that you'd been away so long that no one remembered you. That is not your home, and it is useless to go back there. Maybe it wasn't even Seven-Li Cave, maybe the carter took a wrong turn."

"Are you talking to a dead man?" The carter turned to glare at Binu. "Who says I took a wrong turn? I've driven for years and never once did I take a wrong turn. If I made a mistake, it was with the people. The problem was with the people at Seven-Li Cave."

The strange hearse returned to the road; two oxen and three people, plus an unclaimed coffin.

Surprisingly the early autumn floodwater remained on the ground. The sun shone brightly high above the deserted, bleak public road, which was overgrown with weeds, covered with mud, and full of streams and holes of unknown causes. The hearse was no sooner on the road than it was ambushed by a subterranean hole. The axle snapped and the cart broke into two. The oxen strained to cross the hole, leaving the wheels and the coffin behind in the water, and throwing Binu and the boy in it as well. They crawled onto dry land, only to see one end of Qinsu's coffin sink into the water and the other end about to detach itself from the cart.

Frantically whipping his oxen, the carter complained, "What sort of task did Lord Hengming give me, anyway? First the people give me trouble, then the water and the road, and now it's the turn of you oxen. Just wait and see if I don't whip you to death!"

"Elder Brother," said Binu, "please don't beat them. It's not their fault; the coffin is trying to run away."

"A coffin doesn't have legs," the carter argued as he stared at the coffin in the water. "To hell with you, Qinsu," he cursed. "You were a loathsome man alive and just as loathsome dead, and now your spirit is out to trap my oxcart."

"Don't blame Qinsu's spirit for our difficulties," said Binu. "We've been walking in the sun for three days now, and Qinsu can no longer stay in there, no matter how nice the coffin may be or how wonderful the fragrant herbs are. If he isn't buried soon, they will no longer be able to cover the stink of corruption."

"Who does he have to blame for that? Himself, that's who!" screamed the carter at Binu. "I've transported more than a dozen coffins, but none like this. Someone with karma as bad as that is bound to stink."

146

The carter waded through the water and placed one foot on the coffin. Excessive fatigue and anger lent his face a green pallor. His nose dripped when he spoke, and spittle gathered at the corners of his mouth. He began kicking the coffin. "If you want to stop here, that's your business. You left my cart of your own accord, and there's nothing I can do if you want to leave your corpse out on the open road. Heaven has eyes. I can report back to Lord Hengming that I suffered taking you to Seven-Li Cave." He started pushing down on the cart to help the runaway coffin slip more easily into the pothole.

"We can stop anywhere except on the road," Binu pleaded. "You cannot leave a coffin on the road. The dead man's spirit cannot go into the ground, where it belongs, and people's carts and horses cannot get past."

"That's even better. That's what Qinsu wants. Since he can't move, he doesn't want anyone else to get past." The boy banged on the coffin and burst out laughing. "At long last I've met someone with worse karma than mine. It's one thing for me to forget where my home is, but something else altogether when people in your own hometown won't accept your coffin. Now that is bad karma."

"No matter how bad his karma is, you simply cannot leave his coffin on the road." Binu walked up and grabbed the carter's sleeve. "Elder Brother, you must complete the good deed you began. Since you can't manage with no hands, we'll help you unload the coffin and place it in the field. But please don't leave it on the road."

147

The carter shoved her away, just as the heavy black lacquered coffin sank into the water with a loud sucking noise. The three of them stood frozen to the spot, staring at the coffin, one end in the water, the other end sticking straight up, a lonely object towering over the road like a wayward boulder. That seemed to calm the agitated spirit of the dead man. They could almost hear the sound of water seeping into the coffin.

Wuzhang, the first to recover, came over to press down on the coffin with his foot. "That's good," he muttered. "He didn't jump out, which means he doesn't want to give up such a nice coffin." Then he pushed down hard and said, "So much the better. Qinsu, you cannot accuse me of being unkind or inhumane. You picked the spot. This pothole on this public road is your Seven-Li Cave, and when I pass by here next spring I'll remember to burn some spirit money for you."

There were no travellers on the road; no carts or horses passed by. Once the coffin was unloaded, the two Blue Cloud oxen began grazing by the side of the road, waiting for the carter to put the yoke back on them. But he had to give up trying to fix the broken axle, and he sighed deeply. "Without hands, it's no use. I can drive with my feet, but I need hands to fix the cart." Then, looking towards Blue Cloud Prefecture, he sighed again. "It's all Qinsu's fault. I drove an oxcart out, but now I'll have to return on the back of an ox. I don't know what sort of punishment Lord Hengming will choose for me, but whatever it is, I deserve it."

It was time for them to go their separate ways, a moment that came upon them suddenly.

The boy, sitting on one of the cart planks, wiped a tear from his eye and said, "I don't want to go anywhere. I'm going to sit here and wait for a salt merchant's caravan."

"No salt merchants are likely to pass through a place as remote as this." Binu tried pulling the boy up to take him over to the carter, but he wouldn't budge. So she looked north. "If you have nowhere to go, then come with me to Great Swallow Mountain."

"Only fools go to Great Swallow Mountain," he shouted, feeling humiliated. "You may be a fool, but I'm not. I'd rather die than go to Great Swallow Mountain."

The carter and his oxen stumbled off into the dusk, leaving Binu and the boy on the road. Half of the black lacquered coffin remained submerged in water, the other half was exposed to the setting sun. What had been a splendid and luxurious coffin only yesterday was now spattered with yellow mud and looked utterly dispirited. Since no spirit voice emerged from inside, they could not tell what it wanted done. Perhaps it was unable to be master of the coffin, so Binu decided she would act. She tried to drag the coffin out of the pothole and push it off the road down the slope.

But no matter how hard she tried, it was stuck fast. "Come and help me," she called to the boy. "Qinsu may not have been a nice person, but he was raised by human parents, and we cannot let his coffin remain on the road."

149

"He wasn't raised by human parents. He was no better off than me. Seven-Li Cave, my eye! Old father, old mother, brothers and sisters — ha! A pack of lies. He slithered out through a crack between two rocks, just like me."

"That doesn't mean we can leave his corpse exposed on the road. No one has any say in when and where they are born. Everything depends on your parents and your previous life. But no matter how tough your life is, you need to have a good death and, end up in the ground. If Qinsu just lies here on the road, in his next life he'll either be a dirt clod or a pebble, and people will trample on him all day long."

"I'm not going to help you do anything," the boy said contemptuously. "Only a fool would believe you. All you talk about is the next life. What's so wonderful about the next life? This life has been bad enough. If some stupid woman dares to give birth to me next time, I'll try my hardest to crawl back into her belly and refuse to come out."

The boy would not help, and neither would the spirit. Since Binu could not move the coffin by herself, she gave up trying and walked into the empty field, where she broke off a branch and said to the boy, "You did a fine job digging a grave before. Let's dig one for Qinsu. When men walk by and see a hole, they'll understand. They're strong and they'll move his coffin into the hole."

The boy grinned and pointed at the evening sky. "You'd better stop worrying about Qinsu and get on the road. Haven't you heard that the forest is infested with bandits? If you don't get moving, you may run into them."

"My bundle is gone and all I have left is this mourning robe." She picked up the hem and looked at it. "No, I'm not afraid of bandits."

"You're a woman. If you don't have anything they want, they'll take you."

That gave her something to be afraid about. She rushed back onto the road, where she gazed fearfully at the gloomy fields all around. "Yes, it's time to go. I'll have to leave Qinsu's coffin to some kind-hearted person." She tried to pull the boy up, but he shrugged her hand off.

"Are you deaf? I told you I'm not going to Great Swallow Mountain. I'll wait for a travelling pedlar. When one of them comes along, I'll have food to eat and clothes to wear."

"Do you really plan to sell yourself to a travelling pedlar? They buy old stuff and sell new stuff, but they don't buy and sell people."

"I'm not going to sell myself. Besides, people who sell people don't sell themselves. I have something good to sell, but I'm not telling you what it is." Suddenly, a secretive flame burned in his eyes, which shifted evasively. But only for a moment, until he revealed his secret. "I'm not afraid to tell you. I'm going to sell Qinsu's coffin." He rubbed his hands together as a sign for money. His voice turned shrill. "I'm selling the coffin. The people at Hundred Springs Terrace said that Qinsu's coffin is worth lots of gold!"

Binu was shocked. She clapped her hands over her own ears.

"Why are you doing that? I'm selling Qinsu's coffin, not your ears. You women are always making a fuss. If you think you're being cheated, you can take Qinsu's funeral robe. Didn't you say your husband needs a winter coat? Qinsu's funeral robe is made of silk and satin, just the right gift for your husband."

Binu watched the boy walk up to the coffin and, like a deer, jump onto his new and very large property. Slowly he lifted the lid. "He doesn't stink yet, but if you don't take the robe off now it'll be too late."

Binu turned and ran, not stopping until she spotted some roadside huts flanked by farmers' earthen pots, dogs and chickens. She suddenly realized that she had returned to the human world. She turned to look back down the road. Qinsu's coffin looked like a big, black rock, abandoned there by an unfeeling mountain. On the plain the setting sun shimmered, the last warm rays letting Binu see the outline of a deer. She thought she was seeing things, so she rubbed her eyes and looked again. No mistake. The boy's figure had disappeared, and a deer now stood on Qinsu's coffin.

Five-Grain City

Binu had been told she would see Great Swallow Mountain as soon as she crossed the plain and a mountain range came into view. But she had not expected the plain to be so vast that the end seemed unreachable. Along the way, she passed many heavily populated, bustling cities whose names she forgot, but she could never forget Five-Grain City, where the northbound road ended. Prefecture soldiers formed a dark human wall, driving away carts and people, including Binu.

The road was closed because the King was coming to Five-Grain City. Some people were saying that the King and his entourage had already arrived in Pingyang Prefecture, following a canal that was only rumoured to exist. The day the golden-turret boat was finished, the story went, was the day the canal would open for travel. But everyone in Pingyang Prefecture knew that the golden-turret boat, donated jointly by the three southern prefectures, had already arrived in the capital, while the canal, the construction of which was the responsibility of the four northern prefectures, had yet to be built. No one knew who had had the audacity to deceive the King. A painter had once sketched the canal scene on a scroll, seven feet long, all from his imagination. On it, the masts of hundreds of boats rose like a forest, while the scenery along the way was marked by an abundance of people and animals. The King was moved by the enchanting scene, and the word circulating throughout Pingyang Prefecture was that he and his entourage were travelling south with that scroll, towing the golden-turret boat across Pingyang Prefecture in search of the canal.

Outside the gate of Five-Grain City, people were talking about the deceived King, the lovely scroll, and the golden-turret boat, which had been built by the skilful hands of nine hundred craftsmen. It was the most dazzling sight in the King's procession, or so said the people who lived near the capital. Like a giant dragon among the imperial carriages, it followed the King on his southward journey. Winds blew and clouds gathered wherever it went, leaving a golden aura in its wake.

A child in the crowd shouted out, "There's no canal; that boat will never sail. Heads will roll when the King finds out."

The people by the gate turned to look at the boy and sighed. "If even a child knows what will happen, what is wrong with all those high officials? There's something fishy here."

Another boy, hungry for attention, said, "Canals don't have to be aboveground. What makes you think we are worthy of actually seeing the King's canal? It flows underground, and that's where the golden-turret boat will sail."

His wild talk was met with catcalls. But then, someone pointed to his own forehead and, with his eyes and hands, made gestures that hinted at an even more terrifying rumour — that there was something wrong with the King's head.

"Don't be fooled into thinking that just because you pointed to your forehead and said nothing, you have nothing to worry about," someone cautioned him. "You need to control your tongue *and* your hands. If a constable saw you, you could lose your head as easily from gesturing as from speaking."

Binu listened to all the talk about national affairs, not understanding a word of it. But then she noticed that many of the people were looking up at the city gate, and she followed their eyes. "What are those objects?" she asked. "Are they melons? Why hang them up so high?"

An old man nearby laughed. "Melons? Not the edible kind. Take another look."

She did, and then she shrieked. She raised her sleeve to cover her eyes but her arm slumped and she fell into the arms of the old man, who laid her on the ground. Everyone stared at him.

"I wonder what village she's from," he said, embarrassed and angry at the same time. "A woman of her age, and she's never seen a human head."

A kind-hearted woman came over and gently slapped Binu's face, urging her to open her eyes. "There's no need for someone from a good family to be afraid. Only bandits and assassins are afraid of human heads. Open your eyes and take a good look. Then you'll never be afraid again. You're not going to go blind looking at them. Actually, it will do you good, because you'll be extra careful with what you say and do in the future." In her view, the men deserved to die. Some of the other victims, on the other hand, died a wrongful death, losing their lives because they could not control their tongues.

Binu stared in shock and amazement, unconsciously shutting her mouth to hide her tongue until she needed to take a deep breath. "Elder Sister," she said, "are you warning me by all this talk about losing tongues? How could a few words cost someone her tongue? Back in Peach Village we weren't allowed to shed tears, but after a while we got used to it. But if people cannot gossip, that will turn everyone into voluntary mutes, won't it?"

"It all depends on what kind of gossip." The woman frowned. "What you just said could get you into trouble, talking about voluntary or involuntary mutes. If an official heard you, he might charge you with a crime against the state. In any case, you must control your tongue. Say only what you should say, and not what you shouldn't."

Binu noted that when the woman spoke, her lips moved at the speed of light, but she never showed her tongue.

The big brass bell rang out in the gate tower, a sign for people to enter the city. It induced a sense of panic in people's hearts, but also livened up the indolent crowd. Women called out for their children in shrill

156

voices as the chaotic queue of people ran along beside the base of the wall; apart from the children, no one looked up at the heads hanging on the city wall, as the crowd separated into groups. Not knowing where she belonged, Binu fell in with a group of refugees in tattered clothes. When they reached the gate, they divided again, with the men lining up by a large gate and the women and children by a small one. Binu stood with the women. A soldier came up to look more closely at her nearly-black mourning clothes.

"Who in your family died? How did your mourning clothes get so filthy?"

She was about to answer when she recalled the warning to control her tongue, so she merely pointed to the north. Assuming she was newly widowed, the soldier asked her about the deceased.

"How did your husband die? Was he beheaded by the government for robbery, did he die of the plague during the summer, or did he sacrifice his life at a border as a guard?"

Binu knew that telling the truth would only bring her trouble, but she didn't know how to lie, so she bit her tongue and kept silent, pointing once more to the north.

"Did your husband die up north? Are you a mute? How did we get another mute?" He took a good look at Binu's expression and became suspicious. "That's strange," he said. "Why are there so many mutes on the road today? Get over to the west side. Everyone who is mute, blind, limp, sick or foreign must be examined at the western gate."

The line at the western gate was not long. In front of her stood a candy-seller, dressed in a black robe. From behind, he loomed tall and brawny. He was an unusual sight. Ever since all the young men had been conscripted to work in the north the previous spring, men like this were no longer to be found on the road. They were either working on the Great Wall or working as beasts of burden on the Thousand Year Palace. Binu wondered to herself how this fellow managed to roam the land selling candies, so she stepped out in front to check him out.

He turned to face her and asked, "Big Sister, would you like to buy a candy?"

Binu found herself being scrutinized by a pair of sharp, bright eyes on the man's young but tired face; he was calm as a hawk, yet he embodied an indescribable power to terrify. Shaking her head, she backed away. She remembered those eyes; they belonged to the retainer that the carter had met at Bluegrass Ravine. The masked man had been as tall and as brawny as this one, his eyes as icy cold. She also recalled that a musky smell had come from the masked retainer's black robe. Now a gust of wind blew through the gate, lifting a corner of the man's robe, and Binu detected the same intriguing smell.

She opened her mouth, but was once again reminded of the warning from the woman so she covered her mouth with her sleeve and poked at the man with her finger. He turned around again, but this time his eyes were full of disgust.

158

"Elder Sister, if you don't want to buy a candy, fine, but please don't poke me. I can see you're in mourning, and you ought not to be so familiar."

She turned scarlet from embarrassment, but remained convinced that he was the one who had ridden on the oxcart. Why had he come to Five-Grain City to sell candies? "I wouldn't have poked you if I didn't know you," Binu blurted out, unable to control herself, after all. "Since you are a Hundred Springs Terrace retainer, why have you come here to sell candies? I poked you because I recognize you."

"What's this about? I don't know you."

"You don't know me, but I know you. Big Brother, I have such sharp eyes I can recognize the birds flying over our heads. They fly out one year, and I remember them when they fly back the next. You are going to Great Swallow Mountain too, aren't you? If not, you would not be passing through Five-Grain City. After walking for days, I've finally met someone I know. After the King leaves, let's travel together and look out for one another."

"I am not going to Great Swallow Mountain and I cannot look out for you. I am a cripple. You have two legs but I have only one. How can someone with one leg take care of a two-legged person?" He stared at her coldly, then whipped open his robe and said, "Take a look. I have only one leg. Why else would they have me line up at the western gate to enter the city?"

Filled with doubt, Binu bent down and saw that something was indeed missing under his black robe. He had one good leg and a stump wrapped in cloth. "But you had two legs, I'm sure of that. When you came down from the hills at Bluegrass Ravine, you ran faster than a horse." Binu grabbed hold of the stump to get a closer look and said, surprise in her voice, "It has only been half a month since I left Bluegrass Ravine. How did you manage to lose a leg so quickly?"

"I tell you, I've never seen such a flighty woman. A vulgar woman with an obscene hand. How dare you grab hold of a man's leg!"

Binu felt something hit her hand; he had swatted her with his candy rack. She looked up to see the icy cold stare replaced by a flame of hatred.

"Control your hand," said the man, "and watch your tongue. Let me tell you, with things so chaotic in the city, killing a loose woman would be easier than squashing an insect."

The people who were already inside the gate turned to examine Binu with penetrating stares.

"No matter how hard life is," a female beggar said haughtily, "a woman should not forsake her chastity. Look at her, she has yet to shed her mourning clothes and already she is seducing a man."

A couple who looked like mutes gave Binu filthy looks and gestured angrily, "What a loose woman. Even a bitch in heat knows to pick her place. But not her."

The humiliation brought tears to Binu's eyes. What kind of woman did they think she was? The unanimous evil eye from the crowd frightened her, and now she regretted ignoring the warning of the woman. She should not have opened her mouth so readily in Five-Grain City. It had taken only three comments for

160

them to turn her into a loose woman. Embarrassed and enraged, she felt like following the Peach Village custom of spitting three times at these people, but lacked the courage. So she resigned herself to raising her sleeve to cover her mouth and slinking away into the crowd.

The tower bell had stopped ringing, causing people who wanted to enter the city to make a frenzied surge towards the gate. Still feeling the effects of humiliation, Binu watched their backs and followed behind them, keeping her distance from the mysterious cripple. Over the heads and shoulders of people separating them, she saw the candy rack and the little candied figures swaying happily in mid air. The colourful candied figures — fairies, deities, ghosts and cherubs — sent frozen smiles to Binu.

The sour stench of human bodies and their clothes and luggage permeated the air. Someone coughed and spat up a gob of phlegm. It was a consumptive standing unsteadily behind Binu; clearly influenced by public opinion, he had decided that she was a loose woman. So, after a violent coughing fit, he reached under her robe. At first she didn't scream, but merely slapped his hand away and moved forward after tightening her robe. But he pressed forward, a stick-thin, bony hand and a soft, secretive organ coming together to attach themselves to her buttocks. This time she screamed; her lips moved a few times and tears began to flow. She covered her eyes with her sleeve.

Stumbling and struggling to break free, Binu reached out and touched many people's faces. Wanting to avoid being injured, they stepped back and made way for her.

And so, like a wheel, Binu rolled over next to the man selling candied figures. He stood up when he saw Binu heading straight for him. An agile jump on his one leg took him easily out of her way. Tears were already pouring down her face when she hit the ground. The crowd saw her point at the consumptive man; her lips were moving but nothing came out. All they heard were fragile, baby-like sobs.

"Where did this woman come from?" someone commented, after analysing the crying. "A grown woman should not cry like a baby."

Another woman, moved by what she saw, approached her out of compassion and touched her. "Don't cry," she said. "You mustn't cry once you've entered the gate. It's a Five-Grain City rule, has been for a hundred years."

Binu flicked away all the hands reaching out to her and stubbornly sat on the ground and cried, her tears flying in all directions.

People who were trying to pull her to her feet jumped back, shielding their faces with their hands. "Where did this woman come from: water? She cries like rain; my clothes are all wet."

Binu's wails drew the attention of gate guards, who ran over, shouting, "Who's crying? Who's crying at the gate? Have you had enough of living?"

People frantically moved away from Binu and pointed. "Do something with this woman. A little mistreatment and she cries like rain."

The guards noticed her mourning clothes and saw that the hem of her robe was already submerged in a puddle of water. They yanked her to her feet. "Why have you come here to cry instead of going to the graveyard? Even a three-year-old knows that there are no tears allowed inside the Five-Grain City gate. The punishment is death. A grown woman ought to know that."

"She's just begging to die," exclaimed the consumptive, who had threaded his way back through the crowd. "Her tears have ruined Five-Grain City's excellent *feng shui* and for that she should lose her head."

People stared sombrely at the guards, waiting for something to happen. The guards whispered among themselves for a moment before sending over a young guard with a spear. The crowd's gaze fell on the shiny tip of the spear as he circled her. "They're going to behead her right here. She's going to lose her head."

But someone who knew a bit about beheading was quietly critical of the guard's weapon. "A spear? That won't do it. They need to use an executioner's blade."

In a trembling voice, a woman warned her child, "Be good. Don't get too close, or your clothes will be splattered with blood."

Little by little, doubts were voiced in the crowd. "This doesn't look like a beheading. Maybe they won't do it. No, they won't, they're not going to behead her."

The young guard's next move came as a surprise; he simply lifted the sleeve covering Binu's face with the tip of his spear and studied her tearful face. "Cry, go ahead and cry. We'll let you have a good cry." It was impossible to tell if he was playing with her or truly

163

urging her to cry. The crowd saw him touch her face with his index finger, then stare at it and shout, "Hey, look at this teardrop, it's as big as a pearl. It can stand alone on my finger."

"Looking at it isn't enough," said the other guards. "If it doesn't taste right, it doesn't matter how big it is. Go on, see how it tastes."

The young guard chased away a few adventurous children before warily turning around to put the tear-dipped finger in his mouth. All eyes were on him.

"He's putting tears in his mouth!" one of the surprised onlookers shouted. "What in the world is he doing? Are her tears some sort of delicacy?"

The young guard was focused on tasting the tear; suddenly his nervous tongue stopped working and his knitted brows smoothed out, as an excited light shone brightly in his eyes. "A very good tear," he shouted ecstatically. "A great tear. Not too salty, a trace of sweetness, a bit tart, slightly bitter, also somewhat spicy. It must be the finest tear in all of Five-Grain City."

The other guards jumped for joy. One of them walked up and clapped him on the shoulder. "Well done," he complimented the young guard. "You didn't waste the time you spent in the pharmacy. Thanks to your tongue we have found the best tears in Five-Grain City."

The guards at Five-Grain City were satisfied in the knowledge that they would be rewarded for something they had not done. The crowd had no idea what was happening. A rare beheading, the answer to their prayers, was about to be played out when, inexplicably, it was over and nothing had been done. With disappointment showing on their faces, the mystified people bombarded the guards with questions.

"What happened? Why did you spare the woman? Is this some sort of memorial day for the King? Is he going to pardon everyone?"

Unable to reveal details, the guards hinted that the woman was not destined to die. That answer did not appease the crowd.

"Why was she spared? On what grounds?"

The guards, growing impatient, shouted, "On the grounds that her teardrops are big, on the grounds that her tears have five different flavours. Haven't you heard that the tear soup in Master Zhan's medicinal cauldron is drying up? It's not worth getting excited about. Do we detect a hint of jealousy?"

Under the surprised watch of the crowd, Binu left a silvery trail of tears as she was carried through the gate by the guards. People standing at the front saw them deposit her by a pile of firewood, next to a wheelbarrow.

The refugees by the city gate watched as Binu and the firewood were arranged three times before she had a secure seat on the wheelbarrow. Only her face and a shoulder protruded from the pile. She cried, looking up at the sky, while her body was swallowed up by the firewood. Her tears fell on the kindling like rain, causing some concern that it might not burn. The wheelbarrow was long gone before the people learned that she had not been taken to be used as firewood, that not only had she evaded a calamity, but she was actually being taken to the Zhan Mansion to work. To do what? To cry: to be a weeper. It turned out that the Zhan Mansion was in urgent need of human tears to brew medicine. No one in the crowd could believe their ears, which was only to be expected. A medicine pedlar who had close dealings with the Zhan Food and Medicine Section revealed to the crowd that the dark shadow of illness had settled over the mansion.

Prefect Zhan had sent for a one-time Longevity Palace doctor who had retired to the Pine Forest Temple. Believing that a malignant aura dominated the mansion, the doctor stressed the importance of supplementing and correcting the aura and gave them a prescription whose only special ingredient was tears that contained the five human tastes: bitter, salty, sweet, sour and spicy. Prefect Zhan thought that the doctor was playing with him, but he did not dare contradict him, given the man's high status and excellent reputation, as well as the many difficult and unusual illnesses he had cured for three kings. Prefect Zhan was the most powerful person in Five-Grain City, but all his power and money could not buy as many tears as he needed. He laid down the law to all the officers and soldiers in the city, so that they swore that they would find the saddest woman in Five-Grain city and present him with the largest, best-tasting teardrops of all.

Fortune had smiled on them this day, for they had discovered Binu's tears. Not completely won over, the refugees discussed among themselves the medicinal value of tears. Some wetted their fingers with one of their own teardrops and chased after the young solider who had tasted Binu's tear. But their self-promotions were all rejected. Once the wheelbarrow was on its way, a line of flags was raised high above the guard tower, sending a message to all four city watchtowers. An old man at the city gate, who had been a standard bearer in his youth, read the signal for everyone: "Found the saddest woman. The largest and best tears are on their way to the Zhan Mansion."

Tear Brew

The servants in the Kindling Section made Binu take off her mourning clothes before entering the Zhan Mansion. Slowly she removed her robe, which she held in her arms in the firewood shed as she wept.

A servant came over and said to her, "Don't cry yet. We don't have a tear vat, and you're wasting your tears by letting them fall on the firewood."

They snatched away the robe and threw it on the firewood, but when they saw her tearful eyes fixed on it, they said, "Are you afraid we'll take your robe from you? When they hold a funeral in the Zhan Mansion, even the stone lions wear white robes made of soft brocade. Don't condemn us just because we work in the firewood shed."

Binu continued to stare silently at the robe, inviting a scornful look from the servants, one of whom picked it up with a long stick and put it on the highest pile of wood. "You don't want to part with it, is that it? Very well then, we won't burn it. We'll keep it for you for after you finish crying."

An old man with a long beard came for Binu. Following a strong aromatic scent, he led her to a dark room where the medicine was brewed. A liquid boiling in the cauldron suffused the steamy room with a pungent odour. A cauldron worker tended the fire with great concentration, while another chopped herbs at a table and yet another stirred the mixture in the cauldron. In a corner of the room women and children — boys and girls — sat in the dark, crying into vats that they held in their hands.

"We have a new weeper," the old servant said to someone in the dark corner. "Bring her the biggest vat."

A thick-set woman emerged from the darkness with a vat that was about half her height. "I hear that your tears are large and very fine," she said to Binu. "I'd like to see just how large and how fine."

The other weeping people had also heard that the newcomer had exceptional tears, so, from time to time, they looked up from their vats to appraise Binu, their eyes filled with suspicion and animosity. The servant who was chopping herbs came over and politely gave her instructions: "Take your time and aim at the vat. Stop to rest every once in a while," he said. "No need to cry your heart out. That does no one any good. All we want are your tears. Let me know when you have filled half a vat. We must taste them before adding them to the cauldron."

Binu sat down with the vat in her arms and watched the other weeping people cry into the vats with great precision. Their eyes were dripping like house eaves after rain, and the room was like a strange teardrop workshop. Binu looked around blankly, knowing it was

169

time to start crying, and thinking that Qiliang's winter clothes were still nowhere to be found. Consumed by worry, she was unable to cry.

"My tears are sweet," remarked a boy who had abruptly stopped crying and was glaring at Binu. "What do yours taste like? You adults may have lots of tears but they are bitter, or sour, or salty. You can't shed sweet tears."

Before Binu could reply, a woman sitting nearby said, her voice dripping with envy, "She can shed the best tears in Five-Grain City. Sweet tears mean nothing. She sheds five-flavour tears. I wonder how big a reward she'll get."

"What's a five-flavour tear? There can only be one taste in tears from the eyes. Let me taste one of hers. It must be a hoax." Leaning over to check Binu's vat, the boy was about to reach in with his finger when he saw it was empty. "Why aren't you crying? Don't you know how? Haven't you ever had anything sad happen to you?"

"I know how to cry, child. Many sad things have happened to me; it's just that I can't think of a single one when I sit down to cry."

"You must try. Think about the saddest thing ever. I think about how my father left me in a duck shed and I wasn't found until someone came to gather the eggs. I was covered in duck feathers and duck droppings! Even now people call me Duck Feathers, and my tears flow whenever I think about my name." All the time he was talking he held his vat below his face to catch each falling tear. He continued, "The sweet tears of a child are the rarest, and it takes a long time to collect even half a vat. I have no idea what makes women sad or how to get them to cry. Go and ask those women over there."

The few women who were busy crying were, at first, reserved, but after not hearing any sounds from Binu's vat for some time, they looked up and glared at her.

"Hurry up," one of them said. "You won't be paid until your vat is full. I can tell you have had a rough life, so how can you not have something sad to think about? Close your eyes and you'll be fine."

Thinking that the other weepers were obstructing Binu, the medicinal worker came over to chase them away. "They're waiting for your five-flavour tears at the cauldron," he urged. "A vat from you will probably be as good as five vats from others, so make sure you give it a good cry."

"I want to," said Binu, "I really do, but crying like this is acting and I simply cannot do it."

The worker blinked. "Didn't someone in your family just die? Was it your husband? How will you spend the rest of your life without him? Think about that."

"Don't put a curse on him!" Binu cried out in shock. "My husband Qiliang is working on the Great Wall at Great Swallow Mountain. He's not dead. Please, Sir, spit three times on the ground, please do that for me."

The herbal worker spat three times on the ground and scraped the ground with his foot as an imperceptible smile appeared at the corners of his mouth. "Once he's at Great Swallow Mountain, he'll have only half a life left, whether he's cursed or not."

He looked at Binu and then at the women in the corner. "Your husband isn't the only one there. Just ask those with the bitter tears; ask them how many of their husbands have come back alive."

After a long silence, Binu heard a cacophony of confessions from the women who produced bitter tears.

"More men died mining rocks at Great Swallow Mountain than anywhere else. They had incurred the wrath of the Mountain Deity, who sent avalanches down on those who worked the hardest. My husband was one of them."

"More people died in my family than any others. My husband and three brothers all perished on Great Swallow Mountain. The youngest brother tried to escape but was caught half-way out and was buried alive."

The confessions were followed by pitiful sobbing. Binu left her vat and went up to the Great Swallow Mountain widows. Grabbing the hands of one, she said, "Elder Sister, you said that mining rocks incurred the wrath of the Mountain Deity. My husband Qiliang is building the wall; he won't incur that wrath, will he?"

The widow withdrew her hands and waved them in the air with a sad look. "Those mining the rocks incur the wrath of the Mountain Deity, but those building the wall cannot escape it either. They are all going to die."

Extreme sadness and resentment filled the hearts of the Great Swallow Mountain widows and brought forth an abundant harvest of tears. Splattering sounds emerged from the vats in their arms. Spurred by the sound of that harvest, the older folks, who shed sour tears, and the young women with salty and spicy tears, even the children, with their sweet tears, all began to cry freely. The chorus of wails, accompanied by pained screams, splintered the dark room as weepers aimed their contorted faces at the openings of the vats. Facing this sudden surge of tears, the cauldron and herbal workers did not know whether to respond with joy or with concern; they ran around reminding people to sob, not howl. The herb-chopping worker kept a calm watch over Binu, who was trembling in the midst of all the sobbing. He could see her face, white as a sheet in the dark room; then a silvery light flickered, followed by a gushing of tears.

"Into the vat," he shouted. "Aim at the vat."

But she dropped the vat and stood up. The herb worker watched her stumble out of the room, leaving sprays of tears in her wake. He scooped up the vat and ran after her, rushing up beside her, but was only able to collect a few precious teardrops. Panicking, he dropped the vat and chased after her, but she had already disappeared at the far end of the winding corridor. All he could manage was a shout at her mournful back, "Come back, you'll get seven sabre coins for a single vat of tears."

But seven sabre coins meant nothing to Binu, who was running from the news of death, in such a frenzy that it looked as if she might run all the way to Great Swallow Mountain.

Assassin

Binu considered returning to Five-Grain Tower, where small traders and pedlars from the city, with their reed mats, stoves and kindling, set up stands at the edge of the elm grove, but she was too proud to ask for help. Suddenly she sensed someone watching her; it was the cripple who sold candied figures. His tall figure was like a mountain. In the two days since she'd last seen him, he'd grown much more haggard; his imposing face was now clouded, giving him a gloomy appearance. Binu noticed that his remaining foot was bare, missing the straw boot that most Blue Cloud Prefecture men wore. His once-full candy rack was leaning against the wall; half of the candy was gone, the remaining half looked quite forlorn.

At first she avoided his gaze, unwilling to meet anyone who had witnessed her humiliation. She crouched down and walked away from the wall, but turned around after a few steps. The man's eyes, which had been cold and bright the day before, like the eyes of the people coming down from Bluegrass Ravine years earlier, were now filled with anxiety and sadness; they reminded her of Qiliang in the silkworm shed that summer. The man was not Qiliang, of course, but he was from Bluegrass Ravine, and in Five-Grain City, where she knew no one, running in to a former travelling companion, however indifferent he might have been, was a rare treat. She hesitated for a long moment before walking over. Stopping in front of him, she looked at his bare foot and said, "Elder Brother, you mustn't go barefoot on a cold day like this."

With a glance down the street, he said maliciously, "In a world as big as this, and with so many streets and byways in Five-Grain City, why must you insist on bumping into me?"

Binu glared at him. "How can you say that? Who wouldn't want to bump into a familiar face far from home? This is a public street. What makes you think I meant to bump into you?"

"Watch your mouth! Have you forgotten how it nearly got you into trouble the other day? They carted you away with the firewood then, but today you might not be so lucky. If you don't stop talking, they might drag you to the chopping block."

"Your words are more lethal than poison," said Binu fearfully. "It was your mouth that got me into trouble the other day." She turned and walked off angrily. But then she stopped, turned back, and said, "I wasn't interested in talking to you. I just thought that, since you'd been peddling your goods in town, you might know when the King will arrive and when the road will re-open."

"Go and ask the King when he'll be here," he said, turning to face the wall. "And since I'm stuck here, when the road will re-open is of no interest to me. A child stole my boot. I've travelled on treacherous roads for years, and I never expected that my reputation would be ruined by a little brat."

Binu was still angry. "How can a man get so annoyed over a boot? You know how to talk big, but that's about all you can do!"

"If I told you the things I'd done, you still wouldn't understand. Now, get away from me." He was still facing the wall. "If you've seen a child wearing my boot, tell me; if not, get away from me. You're better off talking to the King of the Underworld than to me. You could lose your life and not know why."

He turned around and whispered to her, "Do you remember North Mountain? Do you remember Lord Xintao? Don't cry out when I tell you who I am. I'm Shaoqi the Assassin, the last descendant of Lord Xintao. My grandfather was responsible for putting the three hundred people of your North Mountain in great danger, which is why I'm trying to spare you. Now please run away as fast as you can."

Binu was momentarily stunned. She could not believe him. Everyone growing up at the foot of North Mountain knew that Lord Xintao had left nothing behind but a large pit on the mountain. Every member of Lord Xintao's family in the three southern counties, from greyhaired old men to newborn babies, had been executed.

Binu cried out, "Be careful, the walls have ears. Elder Brother, you're not frightening me, but you are heading into dangerous territory."

176

People on both sides of the street stuck their heads out to look at them, throwing Binu into a panic.

"I'll be your witness if anyone tries to give you trouble," she said softly. "But you are not Lord Xintao's grandson. You don't know me, but I know you. You are a retainer for Lord Hengming of Blue Cloud Prefecture."

"I *am* Lord Xintao's grandson, and that is why I became Lord Hengming's retainer." His patience exhausted, the man took another look at the cotton carts and snarled, "You think you will be my witness. Well, no one will be your witness if you don't run for your life."

Binu heard him swear, then was shocked to see him raise the candy rack and fling it at her, scattering the small figures to the ground. She screamed and ran down the street, only to be met by a group of constables swarming towards her in black uniforms, some with spiked clubs. She turned the other way, but managed to take only a few steps before some carters jumped down off their cotton wagons and pulled out clubs from the piles of cotton. Mounted soldiers galloped over from farther west, blocking the exits to the street.

At first Binu thought the constables had been sent by Prefect Zhan, but why would he send so many of them just to detain a woman to get tears for medicine? Feeling lost, she stood on the street, watching the constables rush up and grab the candy pedlar. The man in charge barked a command: "Don't let him lean against the wall — he can leap over them. Hold his arms tightly and don't let him fly away."

Amid the startled shouts from weavers, seamstresses and children, the red figures of the constables swallowed up the pedlar, while one of them triumphantly pulled a glinting sword out from the candy rack.

"Assassin! He's an assassin! We've caught the assassin!"

Shouts and cheers erupted on the street. The word assassin sent Binu running, and she heard someone shout, "That woman is his accomplice. Stop her!

Not knowing what else to do, Binu turned and shouted, "I'm not an assassin."

But men were already running towards her. The last thing she saw as she lay on the ground was an upsidedown street, on which fluffed cotton and velvet pieces were floating to the ground, like snow falling from the sky.

Word of an assassin spread through Five-Grain City like the water rushing down its stormy, rain-swept streets. Autumn rain flooded in from the curious south, travelling back and forth between the northern residences of the officials, merchants and rich families and the brothel district in the south. The raindrops, like humans, held their breath and listened in to people's discussions about the assassin.

Men were talking about the assassin, Shaoqi, who had passed himself off as a candy pedlar, but few inquired about the cause of his missing leg; perhaps there were simply too many people with missing arms and legs. They had animated discussions about the false sole of Assassin Shaoqi's boot, which had concealed poison and a dagger, noting the remarkable skill of Blue Cloud Prefecture shoemakers, who could turn the sole of a cripple's boot into an armoury. The assassin's candy rack was an even greater wonder. Despite noting its strange shape, no one had realized that it could be bent into a bow. The assassin had sold his candy figures selectively; those he would not sell held their own secrets: the sugar coat could be cracked open to reveal the arrowheads inside.

Boys were chasing after a young tramp called Abao. People said that the King would have been assassinated outside Five-Grain City if Abao hadn't stolen the assassin's boot, and that the King was going to summon Abao to an audience with him as soon he entered the city. Hence, for the sake of the city's honour, officials had already cleaned Abao up; they had even had a childsize formal silk robe made for him. No one would recognize the boy now, they said; the head lice in his filthy dishevelled hair were picked clean, and the best doctor in town had treated the festering sores at the corners of his mouth so that they no longer attracted flies. But some of the shady characters who had gathered at the foot of Five-Grain Tower were unhappy with the praise lavished on Abao. "That boy's no thief," they said jealously. "All he knows how to do is slip shoes off people's feet."

Shaoqi, the assassin, had slept on his back, unaware of Abao's special talent, which had given Abao the rare opportunity to bring honour to his ancestors. On the previous night, someone had seen him return, complaining about the one-legged assassin's boot. It was a high-quality boot, but since there was only one, he could only sell it to another cripple. The boys said that Abao never tried on the shoes he stole because they stank. But the assassin's boot gave off an unusual musky fragrance, so he stuck his foot in. Being an expert on shoes, men's and women's, he shouted as soon as he tried it on, "There's something inside this boot. It must be sabre coins!"

Some young tramps crowded around to watch him cut the sole open. It wasn't sabre coins; it was three daggers and a packet of poison.

Assassin Shaoqi's reputation had preceded him. Some doubted his royal bloodline, saying that, thanks to the King, Lord Xintao's descendants had all disappeared from the face of the earth. But a nagging question remained: who but Lord Xintao's grandson would harbour such deep hatred for the King and would consider it his mission in life to kill a ruler who was worshipped by thousands of subjects? Speculation centred around the inside story, all about the mastermind behind the assassin. A rumour about Hundred Springs Terrace in Blue Cloud Prefecture, the assassin's home, was already circulating. Everyone was talking about Lord Hengming, how his wealth matched the King's, how he employed several hundred retainers with unusual and esoteric skills, and about the clever devices and secret tunnels that surrounded his residence.

180

"The King will never make it to Five-Grain City," they said. "The country will change hands in the winter, and Lord Hengming of Blue Cloud Prefecture will become the new ruler."

All agreed that Shaoqi was exceptionally talented, for he could shoot a poplar leaf from a hundred paces, retrieve a dagger from his boot in the blink of an eye, and could fly over roofs and walk on walls. But his handsome face, his tall, strong physique, and the fire of wrath that had burned inside him for years, were his greatest hindrances. An assassin can be ugly but must not be handsome. An assassin can be tender but anger is a taboo. There was no greater misfortune than for an angry, handsome man like Shaoqi to become an assassin, which is why he had decided to wear a black robe and a dark bandanna to cover his face, giving him the appearance of a bandit.

"Who would be afraid of anyone hopping along on one leg?" said one of the tramps.

Everyone agreed that the missing leg was as good as a travel permit, that it had allowed the handsome Shaoqi to slip easily into Five-Grain City. But exactly when had he lost his leg, and how? While it was normal for an assassin to assume a disguise, it was certainly unusual for one to do so by cutting off a leg.

An old assassin spoke up, "I wasn't his teacher," he said, "nor was I a retainer at Hundred Springs Terrace, so I don't know how they deal with the custom of living testaments, but I do know that this one was well designed."

His companions questioned him anxiously, "A living testament? What do you mean by that? Are there dead testaments? Don't keep us in suspense."

"When I was young, I did a job for the Sun family in Shepherd Town. I took the money and was ready to leave when someone in the family asked me to leave a living testament behind. That was my first time working for a rich family, so I didn't know what to expect. I thought I'd leave a fingerprint, and stood there waiting for them to bring me the paper. What they brought instead was a copper basin and a knife. They wanted my toes, so that they could trust me completely. When a rich family hires an assassin, they don't just plot against their enemy; they protect themselves against the assassin too. They're afraid they may be implicated if the assassin were to reveal his identity after too many killings, so they ask the assassin to promise that he will stop at some point. Taking a toe from you will not affect your work, but it serves as a daily reminder that you must keep your promise."

The bandit lamented the fact that the world had changed so quickly. Toes had once been enough for a living testament, but now people required a whole leg.

"Shaoqi was different from me," he continued. "He was hired to assassinate the King, and it was an all-or-nothing proposition. His leg was probably more than just a living testament; it would also serve as a way out for Lord Hengming. If Shaoqi's attempt were to be exposed, Hundred Springs Terrace would present the leg to the King and tell him they had discovered the plot and had lopped off one of the assassin's legs to foil his plans. By keeping Shaoqi's leg, Lord Hengming was able to put himself in the clear."

City Gate

The assassin's head did not join the other ones on the city wall, after all; rumour had it that the beheading had been postponed until after the King's arrival. No one in Five-Grain City, except for a few important officials, knew where the assassin Shaoqi was being held, but everyone knew the whereabouts of the woman from Blue Cloud Prefecture. She was being displayed in a cage at the city gate and crowds of people gathered to gawp at her. A downpour sent the guards scurrying for shelter, and the adults gawking at her ducked under the eaves of shops. Seeing that the guards were not paying attention, some youngsters ran through the rain to stare at her. One gave her an ear of corn, then ran back into the crowd to deliver the latest news:

"The assassin is unaware that she ought to be afraid, and the rain doesn't seem to bother her. She's asleep in there!"

Someone explained patiently, "She may not be an assassin. She was born with a big mouth and talked a bit too much with the real assassin. She likes to talk, but after she was caught she could not explain why she'd come to Five-Grain City. She said she had walked a thousand li to deliver winter clothes to her husband, but then she wasn't able to produce any clothing and was considered a suspect. The government put her in a cage to await the King's arrival; when the King comes, the suspect may be released by means of what is called a royal pardon."

When the rain eased up, women came to the city gate in their straw hats. Showing undisguised interest in Binu, some of them wondered how such an honest, respectable looking woman could turn out to be an assassin.

"All women miss their husbands, but none as much as she did. Her feelings must have affected her mind; otherwise, why would she chat with the assassin Shaoqi in front of all those constables?"

Everyone tried to get a look at Binu. But her hands were fixed in a wooden pillory, out of sight, and her dishevelled hair, heavy with raindrops, obscured her face. Some latecomers shouted unhappily to the guards, "You have to provide a better display than this. It's raining so hard that those of us who came late can't see a thing in that cage. At least let us see her face."

Pressed by the crowd, one of the guards came down from the tower with a huge leaf over his shoulder. Reaching in through the iron bars, he tried to tie up Binu's hair, then he poked Binu roughly with his spiked baton to wake her up. "I don't know how you can sleep so soundly in this pouring rain, in a cage, with your hands and head in a pillory. I didn't want to wake you up, but the people won't let you sleep, and there's

185

nothing I can do about it. So stop sleeping. Show yourself, let them see you."

Binu raised her pale, watery face, and the women could see that she had been a pretty young woman whose looks were ruined by fatigue. She opened her eyes under the gaze of many people; she tried to speak, but her mouth was gagged by a mouth bit and she could not make a sound. A pure glow, like moonlight, brimmed in her eyes; the silvery glow slid down her face, brightening the cage and submerging it and her in a bright light. The guard jumped back, as he noticed that a patch of green moss had sprouted under the cage after the downpour, and that specks of rust had appeared on the iron slats wherever her body had touched them. He let out a startled cry. He knew that the cause was her tears, not the rain.

"Stop crying," he said, "tears are not allowed. I know that you feel you have been wrongly accused, but you are not allowed to cry, no matter how great the injustice. I don't care if moss grows under your cage, but I'll be in trouble if it rusts because of your tears. Don't blame me if I treat you harshly, because I will suffer if you keep crying."

Binu looked up at the sky, now bright and blue following the downpour. A few raindrops fell on her face from the top of the cage; they were indistinguishable from her now legendary tears.

"Don't look at the sky," he said. "Look at the ground. Prisoners in cages are not allowed to cry at the sky. That's the rule. Look down at the ground, right now. Do as I tell you."

186

Since Binu was confined by the wooden pillory, it was impossible to tell if she was obeying his command or resisting it. She moved her head slightly and lowered her eyes to stare at the guard, the white light from her tears continuing to flow.

"I told you to look down at ground," he said, rubbing his eyes. "Don't look at me. Didn't I just tell you not to cry? Why are you still crying? They say your tears are toxic."

He ran back to the guard tower, where, apparently, he was reprimanded, for he came down again with a black scarf. He reached into the cage to cover Binu's eyes.

"My superior said your eyes are too dangerous, and we have to keep a close watch on them. You don't need to see anything anyway; it is others that need to see you, as entertainment." Trying to avoid her tears, he moved too slowly and felt a boiling stream of water drench his hand. At that moment thunder rumbled across the sky above the city wall, and a strange commotion erupted among the crowd of onlookers.

A loud thunderclap sounded behind them, and the guard turned to see the silvery light from the cage reveal some hideous-looking evil faces. Many in the crowd lost control of their knees and fell to the muddy ground, knocked over by the invisible tide of tears. Onlookers nearby did not move away quickly enough to avoid being sprayed. "Why is this water so hot?" they shouted in alarm. "How could autumn rainwater be this hot?"

Wrongdoers were collapsing to the ground, crying their eyes out, slapping and beating their chests, but refusing to reveal why they were crying. People who had led a moral life were rewarded by being able to withstand the impact; hands remained in sleeves for those who were used to doing just that; people who like to bend forward while standing remained crooked as a willow tree; and hands roamed the bodies of those who liked to scratch themselves. It was this group of people who managed to maintain a vestige of dignity on behalf of the citizens of Five-Grain City. Moving among the evil bodies of those who had cried out their regrets, they praised each other.

"You've led a blameless life," they said. "See, the water has wet your robe, but that's all. We have nothing to cry about." Pleased with themselves, they calmly observed the area around the city gate, searching for the source of the sudden storm of tears. They noticed a torrent of water rushing beneath Binu's feet; narrow and clear, it surged rapidly with a cold glint, like watery arrows firing at the crowd. They concluded that the tear-storm resulted from that torrent, and that the curse of tears had originated from the Blue Cloud Prefecture prisoner.

They looked up and saw that the guards on the wall were playing finger guessing-games behind the battlements, completely oblivious to what was happening below. The guards' nonchalance reminded someone that the solution was to move to higher ground. Everyone, innocent or not, would be safe once they were higher up than the woman.

Slowly people regained their senses and began searching for the nearest higher ground, warning onlookers, "Don't get too close to that woman. The assassin from Blue Cloud Prefecture brought a curse of tears, and you cannot know what sort of calamity will befall you if you come under its spell."

Some children had climbed a tree to get away from the dangerous water on the ground. A woman with lithe, strong legs wrapped her arms around a tree and began to climb, but had not made it far up the tree before a schoolteacher told her to get down, "No matter how much a woman like you is enjoying the scene, you cannot climb a tree. It's inappropriate for a woman to do that."

Being fearful of the teacher, the woman slid back down and unhappily smoothed down her robe. "Everyone else can climb trees," she complained. "You men can, so can the children, even chickens and dogs. But not us. First you tell us to get to higher ground, then you won't allow us to climb trees. Where exactly do you expect us to go?"

Thinking of the prisoner, the schoolteacher bemoaned his lack of knowledge. "I have learned something new today, something I cannot explain. How have a little woman's tears managed to cause such an emotional uproar?" Stroking his long beard, he sighed and said, "I don't know how or why this happened."

Suddenly, a commotion broke out near Five-Grain Tower; guards were running around attending to flagpoles. People formed human ladders next to the shops, children in the trees climbed to higher branches.

A frenzied cheer echoed through the square in front of the gate entrance; the shouts rose and fell: "The golden-turret boat is here. Come and see the golden-turret boat. The King is here!"

The canal had yet to flow to Five-Grain City, yet the golden-turret boat had arrived. The King's servants were towing it across dry land. Yes, the King had arrived, and the people crowded in front of the teahouse to gaze at the road, where birds were scared into flight and the edge of the sky was shrouded in a golden light. Through the misty golden fog, they saw the coiled dragon mast of the renowned golden-turret boat, and the crowd spontaneously broke into ecstatic, joyous applause. In the opinion of one sharp-eyed individual, the King's long, winding caravan looked like a beached dragon. The splendid coiled dragon mast was motionless, except for the black Nine Dragon flag with its gold piping, which flapped high in the rain-washed sky.

"Nothing is moving," the man said, "not the wagons or the horses or the boat. Could they be stuck?" He was immediately met with angry glares.

"You must be referring to your own broken-down donkey cart. Those are the King's wagons and the King's golden-turret boat. How could they be stuck?"

King

All of Five-Grain City held its breath as it awaited the King's arrival. Above the city gate the Nine Dragon flag flapped in the wind; beneath the gate throngs of people with gongs and drums lined up against the city wall to form the two characters, "Long Life", while the Guo Family Troupe, renowned for its lion dancing, brought out all its dancers. From a charity granary set up by the government came the fresh fragrance of rice, attracting hordes of people, who queued up with their bamboo baskets to wait for the granary to open and distribute Mercy Rice. On the deserted side of the stone terrace, a pair of executioners in red robes stood quietly by the prisoner's cage with aloof, calm expressions; the blades in their hands gave off a sharp, cold glint, seemingly impatient for the time to come.

Lining both sides of the gate entrance were officials from Five-Grain City in yellow or crimson official robes. From a distance the lines appeared harmonious, but a closer look revealed struggles over position and placement. Some believed that their place in the line did not match their official position; unwilling to stand behind others, they moved to more prominent places, encroaching upon others who maintained their places with their elbows and knees. It took the timely interruption by Prefect Zhan for the pushing and shoving to stop and for the gate entrance to recapture its proper solemnity.

But the waiting was interminable, and suspicion grew. The officials began to whisper among themselves, staring at Prefect Zhan with a distrustful eye.

"The King may not be here yet," they said, "but the palace vanguards ought to have arrived. Or, at the very least, the King's Dragon Cavalry. If they'd decided not to enter the city, they'd have sent a palace official, so where is he?"

Anxiety was written all over Prefect Zhan's face, where a nagging apprehension had produced a tortuous cold sore at a corner of his mouth, making him moan constantly. A palace official had turned and left immediately after entering town. Unable to ward off any more questions, Prefect Zhan finally let slip the first piece of news concerning the King, "I thought the man was here to deliver a message from the King, but it turned out he just wanted some rotten fish. I asked him why, since they were about to enter Five-Grain City, where the King could have all the fresh fish he wants. Why rotten fish? He wouldn't tell me."

Puzzled by the news, the officials stared wide-eyed, saying that the King was, after all, the King, with tastes that common people could not comprehend. Many of the secrets about Longevity Palace sounded outlandish, and perhaps rotten fish was a recipe for longevity.

After departing with a cart-load of rotten fish, the palace official did not return, leaving behind an oppressive air of suspense. Prefect Zhan sent someone up the city tower to gauge the movements of the King's entourage. He repeatedly instructed everyone on the proper welcoming ceremony, to the point of losing his voice, until finally they had memorized the intricate details, procedures and rules: as soon as the coiled dragon mast began to move, the gongs and drums were to be struck, the lions were to start dancing and the granary would open to distribute Mercy Rice. When the King reached the city gate, the executioners would raise their blades and ask if the prisoner should be beheaded. Normally, the King would respond from his dragon seat, "Stay the knife and spare the prisoner." That was the only detail that worried Prefect Zhan. No one could either imitate the King's voice or predict his mood, so it was impossible to rehearse the ritual for celebrating the King's benevolence. They had to wait until the time came. The ceremony must be polished and distinguished, since all arrangements followed the laws and rites of Longevity Palace, supplemented by the local cultural rules of Five-Grain City. It would make little difference if the weather did not work in their favour. The road would still be muddy in any case after the recent rain, so the King's horses and wagons would travel on a street sprinkled with grain husks and grass ashes; they would arrive at the yamen gate and enter the palace through an underground tunnel.

Everything was in place, except for the King. The news from the tower remained depressing: the King's entourage lay unmoving on the public road like a beached whale. The sentry even said that cooking smoke was rising from the public road, which meant that the King's men were preparing their meals out in the open.

Prefect Zhan felt a cold sweat creep over his body; the fact that the King's men were preparing their own meals was a nightmarish development. He began worrying about the King's opinion of Five-Grain City: had someone maligned their citizens to the King? Did the King have a poor opinion of Five-Grain City? That would indicate a negative opinion of him. Had he been denounced by someone and incurred the King's wrath? Who would that someone be? He cast an inquisitive gaze over colleagues lined up in the entrance and was met by their return gazes. The looks on their faces covered the full spectrum: some appeared muddle-headed, others cunning; some wanted to say something but didn't, others showed off their cleverness by pontificating about the news of the King cooking in the open.

"He is a great king," they said, "for he passes by Five-Grain City and does not want to enter the city to eat a single morsel of the common people's grain."

Finally the sound of horses' hooves shattered the silence on the road. All of Five-Grain City cocked its ears and listened. When three cavalrymen galloped up, someone noticed that they were carrying not the Nine Dragon flag, but a white streamer of coarse material. A thunderous sound erupted. "Kneel down. Everyone kneel down. The King is dead. Long live the King!"

Deathly silence reigned at the city gate, followed by the collapse of mountains of panic-stricken people. "The King is dead, dead!" Those on the edge of the mountain were able to quickly kneel down, but not those in the middle, who could not find enough room for their knees in the narrow space. So they knelt on others' legs and backs. No one dared utter a word, so conflicts erupted in silence and were resolved in the same manner, as an undercurrent of suppressed panting and cursing spread throughout the crowd. Some fought quietly, grabbing and scratching as best they could on their knees until someone cried out, "The King is dead, and my eyes are blinded."

No one knew who the cry belonged to, but it had shattered the solemnity of the moment, quickly turning the sea of humanity into a raging ocean. People forgot that they needed to remain sombre and quiet. Instead, they began excitedly voicing their opinions about the King's death. One shrill, somewhat hoarse voice spoke the minds of many in the crowd and attracted considerable attention: "The King died from being deceived by the officials," he said. "They gave him a false report so that he would travel south to see the canal. But where is the canal? Where is the landing? Where would the golden-turret boat enter the water? Who knows how much he suffered travelling south with that big boat. Can a boat sail in a wheat field? Can it sail in a ditch? The beautiful, big golden-turret boat had to sail along the ground. How could the King not be angry? He did not just die, he died of anger, I know he did."

Shared sorrow prompted the people to disregard the spies around them and courageously express anti-government views. Many even shouted angrily at officials standing at the gate entrance.

The refugees around the granary, too, were getting restless, and a disturbance was quietly brewing as surprise at the announcement of the King's death gave way to concern about the distribution of the Mercy Rice. The hungry refugees were kneeling on the ground, but their hearts had already crept into the granary. Finally one intrepid individual, claiming it was uncomfortable to kneel on someone else's leg, decided to move up a bit. With his basket over his head, he stealthily inched towards the granary.

"Don't climb so high," someone reminded him, "or they'll think you're an assassin and arrest you."

Not bothering to conceal his intentions, he said, "High or low, it's still kneeling. The King is dead, so why worry about assassins now? We need to worry about the government. If they cancel the Mercy Rice, we'll all return home with empty baskets."

He had put into words what was on everyone's minds. Some of the others responded by standing up. "I can't kneel here any longer," they said. "I'm going to kneel over by the granary."

Before the soldiers and officials guarding the granary could react, the reed mat walls around it collapsed under the weight of the surging crowd, and the newly milled rice cascaded down on them. Some ran over to claim the rice, but realizing that they could only scoop up a small amount, they lay down and covered the rice with their bodies. Greed was in evidence everywhere: though their baskets were full, people continued to plough towards the centre of the rice mountain. Some jumped over others' shoulders, some stuffed rice in their shoes when their hands were inadequate, and some shouted at their children to stuff rice up their robes. Older folks, left behind in the free-for-all, shook their baskets impatiently and demanded that the officials come to re-establish order. But Prefect Zhan, along with his underlings, had been so shaken by the crushing news that what was occurring at the granary did not interest them.

As for the three cavalrymen, two seemed utterly deflated, while the third took in his surroundings with concern. Claiming to have grown up in Five-Grain City, he got down from his horse and knelt before Prefect Zhan, quietly enquiring about some property his family had left behind in Five-Grain City.

"You have been serving the King in Longevity Palace," said Prefect Zhan, "so why are you worried about a rundown house out here?"

The man replied, "I am afraid I cannot return to Longevity Palace, and the only shelter from the elements I have is that run-down house."

Prefect Zhan knew there was more to it than that and, nagged with doubt, he disregarded the taboo of speaking about a fallen ruler and asked the cavalryman how the King had died. What came out of the man's mouth was shocking, "The King died three days ago on the road," the cavalryman revealed. "Rotten fish and stinking shrimp could no longer mask the stench from his corpse." News of the King's death had already begun to spread, threatening chaos in the land. The Nine Dragon flag in Longevity Palace had been replaced by the White Tiger flag, and the King's brother, Chengqin, was now sitting on the throne.

Binu

No one in the crowd had been concerned about having to kneel in mud; but there were so many knees and so many rear ends, and so little room, that it led to silent wranglings over space. A few young girls, who foolishly worried too much about their new robes, complied with reluctance and complained loudly. One of them pointed to the caged prisoner and muttered, "Everyone else is kneeling, why isn't she?"

The girl's mother slapped her. "My little ancestor," she said menacingly, "there are plenty of people to envy, but she cannot be one of them. If you don't want to kneel, if you think it's too uncomfortable, why not climb into that cage and stand there with the assassin?"

The forgotten Binu was indeed the only person left standing. Her legs were bound to the iron slats, so she could not have knelt even if she'd wanted to. The soldiers by the city wall had laid down their weapons and fallen to their knees. Even the executioners had put away their blades and knelt beside the cage. The King was dead, and everyone was required to kneel, even ducks and chickens, but not her. She remained standing, waiting for someone to discover the omission,

199

but no one did, except for the little girl. Or maybe they did, but didn't dare say so, since they were required to keep their eyes lowered, and were afraid that someone might ask how they had discovered the omission if they hadn't looked up.

The hearse carrying the dead King had not moved, so the people continued to kneel facing the road. Since the cage stood between them and the road, it looked as if the citizens of Five-Grain City were prostrating themselves before a cage. A crow flew off from Five-Grain Tower and passed overhead; an ignorant bird, it thought that the people were kneeling to Binu, so it circled in the air above the prisoner, cawing its respect. She did not understand the bird's call, but she sensed its emotion, believing that the caws voiced feelings for the kneeling crowd. "Binu, Binu, those people kneeling at your feet are asking your forgiveness." It was not clear if the idea had come from the crow or from herself, but it startled her nonetheless. She wanted to look away, to gaze at the sky or the city wall, anywhere but at the countless knees, but the pillory obstructed her movements. Since she could not turn her neck, she shut her eyes, which prompted tears to flow. Considering her status, she thought this would not be a good time to be crying. Other people were crying on their kness, but she was standing and so it was inappropriate for her to be crying too. So she opened her eyes and forced herself not to look at the knees or the lowered heads. What then should she look at? Perhaps their robes. She could not forget her mourning robe, which had been taken from her at the

200

Zhan mansion, and she wondered who was wearing it at that moment.

Binu told herself to stop thinking about the robe. The Kindling Village sorceresses had predicted that she would die on the road, but there had been few details in their prediction. They hadn't said to her, "You will die shorn of all possessions and the winter robe will never reach Qiliang. Your Qiliang is doomed to have nothing to cover his back, unless he has learned how to turn the yellow sand of the north into thread and weave it with rocks from Great Swallow Mountain." Standing there in her prison cage, Binu was terrified by her thoughts of Qiliang.

A Great Swallow Mountain widow in Five-Grain City had once told her not to think about him all the time. "You poor woman," she had said, "thinking about him is also suffering. You think about him every day and every day he suffers."

One of the weepers in Prefect Zhan's mansion had also warned her, "Be careful with your dreams. Don't ever dream about going to see your husband. With your luck, the person you dream most of seeing will suffer just like you."

So Binu cleared her mind of thoughts of Qiliang, forcing herself to think instead about the pampered body of the King and wonder where it was lying, in a coffin or on the golden-turret boat. What were his funeral clothes made of, gold or silver? Were there King's marks on his wrists? She suddenly realized that she had substituted the King for the thief Qinsu, with his small eyes and ratty beard. She would never know if the King had the word "King" tattooed on his wrists. She felt unspeakable regret, not over her life and death, but the King's. Who among the commoners did not want to see the King with their own eyes? She had wanted to look at his face and his wrists. But the King was dead.

Anger welled up inside the two executioners as they knelt alongside the cage. At first they quietly complained about the King's untimely death, which had cost them the once-in-a-lifetime opportunity to perform the ceremony they had rehearsed so many times. In the past, they had been rewarded whether the prisoner was executed or not, but now they would receive nothing; and, given the chaos at the gate entrance, who would be interested in watching them chop off someone's head now? When the commotion broke out at the granary, one of them had begun sharpening his sword with a violent ferocity, while the other had simply stood up and stretched before kneeling again.

"Looting is not our responsibility," he said, "that's for the constables to deal with, so let's just kneel here."

Soon they saw some of the officials filing out through the gate entrance and heard someone shout, "Hey, why are they leaving, when we're still here? Being good citizens has cost us our Mercy Rice."

One of the men said defiantly, "Let's not kneel any more. Let's get up. Why should we keep kneeling now that the officials have fled? What's the point? Get up, everybody, get up. All the Mercy Rice is gone, but there's plenty more at the rice shop. Let's go and get it."

At this point, the executioners could no longer contain themselves. They stopped one of the officials, who was running their way. "Are we going to use these swords today or aren't we? Tell us, or we'll join the crowd looting the rice shop." Getting no response, they walked off with their swords, still in their red uniforms. One of them followed the mob to the rice shop, while the other was caught and beaten by some angry old men and women, who pulled and grabbed him, crying and cursing, "You have chopped off too many people's heads, and we're not going to let you go today. Cut off our heads if you dare."

The executioner raised his shiny sword high above his head and ran off. "Don't think the world has changed," he shouted. "The old King is dead, but there's a new King. Tomorrow I will start beheading people for the new King."

Binu stood alone in her cage and watched as the executioners disappeared in the rioting crowd. The crowd swallowed up the officials and soldiers, and no one had any thoughts for the prisoner. She wondered if anyone would remember her. She felt like shouting, but her mouth was still gagged; she wanted to leave the cage, but her body was still confined by the pillory. She watched people emerge from the rice shop and disappear into the nearby fabric and blacksmith shops. Someone came out with a farm tool in his arms, bright red blood streaming down his face, the result of a fight over a hoe. Another man carried a bolt of silk, but it was quickly shredded by other hands and, by the time he broke free, all that was left on his shoulder was the wooden roll.

The uproar stirred Binu's blood as she watched, and she heard herself shouting directions, "Go over to Used Clothes Street. Get their winter clothes. Get me a set of winter clothes for Qiliang." Her voice burst out of her frail body, and she shut her eyes, as a fresh teardrop rolled out of the corner. She knew it was a tear of shame.

Binu stood in the cage, waiting for the rioting crowd to remember her. She knew that the pillaging would come to an end at some point. She could only wait for someone to loot her cage. Finally some boys from the area below Five-Grain Tower came running towards the cage. One held a rock, another a scythe he'd stolen from the blacksmith's shop. The flames of plundering burned brightly in their eyes. They hacked and beat at the cage, until it gave way. One boy grabbed Binu and began chopping at the pillory. Seeing that she wasn't helping, he tore the black cloth out of her mouth and stuffed it in his pocket. "Why don't you move a bit?" he said. "I'm trying to save you, so stop acting like a corpse."

So Binu began screaming in time with the boy's hacks with the scythe, and she was still shrieking when the pillory was removed. They tried to force her out of the cage.

"Foolish woman, why won't you come out? We're going to sell this cage, so get out. You're free to go."

She felt like sitting down, but her waist refused to bend. Perhaps she had been standing in that narrow cage so long she'd forgotten how to sit. Holding onto the bars, she looked around, then started off towards the city wall, but could only take a few steps. Slowly she retreated to the cage to lean against the bars for support. That, of course, made it hard for the boys to remove it.

One of the boys pried her hands off and said, "Foolish woman, can't you bear to part with the cage? Standing in here has dulled your mind."

They dragged her towards the city gate. "Everyone else is plundering," they said. "Why aren't you? Go and get something for yourself."

Binu was bundled into the crowd, where she stepped on someone's toes. She was caught up in a frenzied mob; people pushed her from behind and elbowed her from in front. The faces on everyone — men and women, young and old — burned red from the thrill of plundering; their breath was fast and shallow, their eyes shone brightly. One person choked on tears as he vowed to loot everything in Five-Grain City. He would burn down the city and kill everyone; no one would survive.

Binu followed some boys into Used Clothes Street. Stumbling as if walking in her sleep, she was different from the other, more excited looters. When she reached a corner, she fixed her gaze on a clothes stand, her eyes full of expectation and shame. The woman who sold used winter robes was stunned by the disaster that was unfolding. Madly waving a forked pole, she wailed as she tried to protect her stock. The boys, with the help of older folk, snatched the pole away from her and pushed her down on a hemp sack, where she was ordered not to resist.

"Come and get it," a boy called out to the others. "It'll be cold soon, so concentrate on the warm clothes."

The clothes on display and the pile of shoes, hats and socks disappeared in a flash. Everything but a single black robe with green piping that had fallen behind the hemp sack. Binu stepped away from the looters and, seeing that no one was watching, bent over to pick up the robe. But too late. Someone else had grabbed a corner; it was the clothes seller, who had somehow escaped from the boys and freed one hand to clutch Binu. She stared at Binu with angry eyes. Binu could not be sure if the woman recognized her as the prisoner in the cage; but she easily spotted Binu's poverty.

"The world has been turned upside down!" she screamed. "People have taken to stealing used clothes! The poor robbing the poor. Well, everyone will be poor again in the next life." Tears streamed down her face as she railed against heaven and earth, but held on tightly to Binu, as if prepared to die with her. She spat on her captive.

When Binu wiped the spittle from her face, tears welled up in her eyes as she said to the woman, "Big Sister, don't hold me like that. Let me go."

"I will not let you go," the woman screamed. "I'll die first, unless you release the robe."

Binu stood there not knowing what to do, when she heard two boys say to her as they pushed the woman down again.

"Are you demented? The forked pole is there under your foot. Pick it up and hit her. She'll let go then."

Still gripping the robe, Binu looked down at the pole and hesitated briefly before picking it up and hitting the woman's hand with it. But the woman was relentless.

"You're that prisoner!" she shouted. "You escaped from the cage, but instead of taking your anger out on the officials, you come here to beat me. You don't know how to rob the rich, so you come here to steal used clothes from me. You're worse than dogs and pigs, all of you!"

Binu was shocked by the venom in the woman's words.

"Don't just stand there," someone said from behind. "Beat her."

So Binu hit the hand again. This time it hurt so much that the woman began to wail, but still she wouldn't let go. Now she remembered Binu's story.

"You're taking my winter robe for your husband. Well, it's no use. Your husband died at Great Swallow Mountain. He's dead, dead. He doesn't need a winter robe any more."

The curse made Binu so furious that she gave the woman's hand a vicious whack with the pole, forcing her to let go. But she didn't stop there; she hit her over and over until one of the boys told her to stop.

"She's let go of the robe. Take it and leave."

Throwing the pole away, Binu ran out onto the street with the robe; now she was crying. After a few steps, she stopped to look back at the woman with remorse in her tearful eyes. Then she ran to the other side of the street, where she stopped and looked back at the boys as if to express gratitude. But it was not the sort of gratitude that can be spoken, so in the end she thanked no one. She simply ran off.

The boys watched as Binu disappeared around the corner of Used Clothes Street. They were fortunate enough to hear the last weeping sound she left in the street, but they could not have cared less. They had never had anything good to say about tears. What was the point of crying?

"Rain moistens the land," the boys said. "The river provides for people, the water in ditches nourishes weeds, and the water in ponds makes fish and shrimps grow big. Only human tears are useless; they are the most worthless things in the world."

The North

Travellers inundated the public road like a flood and divided off in two directions outside Five-Grain City. One group, comprising fancy carriages and magnificent horses, surged towards the clean south, the other, consisting mainly of refugees, headed north like migrating crows.

They passed the beached golden-turret boat, whose gigantic body had now turned into a pile of oddly shaped wooden planks that littered the roadside. The King's entourage had finally left with his corpse and the priceless Nine Dragon golden mast; the boat looked like a fat, tasty fish after a feast, only its bones left behind. Along with the disassembling of the golden-turret boat went the people's fantasy about a journey on the canal. Most of the refugees had never seen a boat and were convinced that it ought to have wheels. Others believed that it had been made in the image of a fish, so it must have a mouth, fins and scales. They actually did discover some painted fish scales on the sides, and a group of people who had gathered around the boat were using hammers to chip them away. They were tight-lipped about what they were doing, but a voluble young boy stopped people on the road and persuaded them to help with the work, telling them there was gold in the paint.

A madman excitedly ran into the oat field, pointed a twig at a pile of excrement and shouted at the flow of traffic on the road, "Come and take a look. The King's shit. Here's the King's shit."

The riot at Five-Grain City had bestowed two pieces of property on Binu: a man's black robe with green piping and an unripe gourd that she had picked up somewhere. She put the loose man's robe over her own and tied the gourd to her sash. Then she pulled her hair into a topknot and gathered the loose strands together with a blue ribbon, which made her look like a willow swaying in the wind-blown sand. Some people caught up with that willowy figure and, on closer inspection, realized that she was the caged prisoner.

"What a lucky woman," they said. "Only yesterday she was waiting to be beheaded, and now she's travelling with us."

Seeing the gourd at her waist, a child asked for some water to drink. Binu shook the gourd to show that it was empty. "My gourd isn't for carrying water," she said. "It will contain my soul if I should die on the road."

"The sword was poised over your neck," they said, "yet you didn't die. Then, thanks to the riot, you have escaped from the cage. But instead of thanking people for saving your life, you keep travelling alone." A fake hunchback in the crowd asked, "Where are you going, anyway?"

"To Great Swallow Mountain. I'm taking winter clothes to my husband. Do you know how far it is from here?"

"Not too far, just another ninety li or so, but you may never get there stumbling along. Take a look at yourself in the ditch water. You are not well. You ought to find a village and rest for a while. My home village is only ten li from here."

"I cannot rest," she said. "The weather will turn cold any day now, and I must deliver this winter robe to Qiliang before the first snowfall."

"Your Qiliang? Who knows if he's a man or a ghost now? Seven out of ten people who went to build the wall are dead, and the remaining three are coughing up blood. The colder it gets, the more they cough. They've all nearly coughed themselves to death!"

"Big Brother, spit three times on the ground. Hurry. You mustn't curse like that." Binu looked daggers at him. "My Qiliang is alive and well. He's used to hard work so he won't get tired or cough up blood."

"Fine, your Qiliang is a man of steel. Others cough up blood but not him." The hunchback spat three times, but reached out to grab her shoulder. "What an ungrateful woman! I was worried about you. In bad times like this, who can be bothered about the bonds between husband and wife? Many Great Swallow Mountain widows went off with someone else. Only a foolish woman like you would struggle against this wind-blown sand to deliver winter clothes."

The man's glibness failed to disguise his lewd intentions. Binu shrugged off his hand and stood to the side, where she waited until he walked away unhappily. An old man turned and gave her an approving smile. "It's a good thing you didn't go with him. He's in the business of tricking and selling women; he was going to sell you to be the wife of a madman."

Speechless, Binu followed the old man for a while. "Old Uncle," she said, "do you know if they'll still be building the Great Wall now that the King is dead?"

"Why not? The old King may be dead, but there's a new King on the throne. All kings want to build walls."

"Old Uncle, I have another question. Why are so many people talking about coughing up blood? I don't believe it. If everyone coughed up blood and their health was ruined, who would build the Great Wall?"

"Those who cough up blood, of course. When I was young, I helped build Dragon Pot Pass and I coughed up plenty of blood on the mountain. You've never been there, have you? You'd know what I mean if you had. When the sun shines on the walls, the rocks turn red, blood red, which is why we call it Bloody Pot Pass." He chattered away until he noticed Binu's ashen face and stopped to try to comfort her. "Coughing up blood isn't so bad; poor people have lots of blood. Didn't I live to come down from Dragon Pot Mountain? There's a trick to hard work: those who know it hide their strength in such a way that the foreman can't tell, but those who don't know it fail to conserve their energy. Everyone who coughed up blood and died did not know how to conserve energy. Is your husband the honest type?"

212

"Yes, he is. My husband Qiliang is the most honest of all the honest men at the base of North Mountain." Binu was overcome by near despair and fell to her knees, giving the old man an opportunity to pick up speed as if ridding himself of a burden. He muttered to himself as he walked away, "Who told you to marry an honest man? Things don't turn out well for honest men."

The old man may have had weak legs, but he walked faster than Binu; he quickly disappeared into the sandy wind, plunging her into a nightmare of despair. Standing on the road, she found she could not move. Another group of people emerged from the airborne sand, all women, with green or pink scarves covering their faces. They walked in single file, with the younger ones leading and the older ones bringing up the rear. What was puzzling was that each of them was carrying a large rock in her arms. When they saw Binu standing motionless in the middle of the road, they said, "Don't just stand there. In such a strong wind, you need to keep moving if you're going to get somewhere. If not, then move out of the way."

Binu stepped aside, nearly knocking the rock out of a woman's arms. The woman was about to scream at her, but recognized her face in spite of the blowing sand.

"Aren't you the woman from the cage? Everyone says you're delivering winter clothes to Great Swallow Mountain. Why are you standing here? Was your husband hit by falling rocks?"

Binu began to sob. "No," she replied. "My husband Qiliang doesn't know to conserve his energy when he works, so he must be coughing up blood."

"He's the one coughing up blood," said the woman, "not you. So why stand here like an idiot?"

"All my internal organs ache when he coughs up blood, and I cannot take another step."

"It's just a little blood," said the woman nonchalantly. "When a man is up on Great Swallow Mountain, he can't worry about blood. The most important thing is to stay alive. All the men from our River Village are there too. See how many of us got together to go to Great Swallow Mountain?"

Binu's eyes lit up, but quickly darkened. "That's wonderful for your village. But I am the only woman from Peach Village who was willing to go." She reached out to tug at the sash on the woman's robe. "Big Sister, please tell me how I can keep my husband alive."

"Go and get a rock," said the woman. "You can't go there empty-handed. People along the way know how you feel, but the Mountain Deity doesn't. Get a rock and walk the sixty-six li to give it to the Mountain Deity at Great Swallow Mountain. He'll see you and will protect your husband, who then won't have to worry about a thing, even if the mountain crumbles and the earth splits open. No rocks will fly at your husband's head."

From Peach Village to River Village, it was the first time Binu had encountered travellers on their way to Great Swallow Mountain. But the women would not let her join them, either because they didn't want a woman who had been imprisoned with them, or because they were afraid she might become a burden. By the time Binu had found a rock and returned to the road, the River Village women had disappeared in the sandy wind. Cradling her rock, Binu ran after them, but only briefly. She knew they could not have got far, but she could not see the pink or green scarves. The wind had sent off the last few northbound travellers, leaving her behind on the sandy road. Weak sunlight filtered through the sand to cast her shadow on the road, a lean shadow, like water that can flow nowhere. It looked like the shadow of the last person on earth.

Cradling the rock, Binu began heading north alone, again. The rock kept getting heavier, as if she were carrying a whole mountain. Rocks of various sizes littered the roadside, and she thought she should pick up a smaller, lighter one until she recalled the River Village woman's words that the Deity at Great Swallow Mountain could see the rock in her arms. The wind was like a galloping horse that had broken free of its reins and, now caught and pulled back by the sun, had stopped its sandy howl. Pale golden sunlight returned, revealing the savage, vast outline of the plain. In the distance, the greyish shadow of a mountain blocked out half the sky. When Binu saw it, she stopped and gazed in happiness at Great Swallow Mountain. The Mountain Deity must be hiding in a crevice, watching her. She had not yet reached Great Swallow Mountain, and she wondered why the rock in her arms could not contain itself any longer. Warmed by her arms, it fell like a landslide and crashed at her feet.

Binu felt no pain. She poked her right foot with her finger, but felt nothing, so she picked up a stick and poked it again. Still no feeling. She knew that her right foot had betrayed her. The left foot had been spared by the rock, but it too would not obey her. Beating her left foot with the stick, no matter how hard she tried, she could not awaken in it a desire to walk. She was determined to move forward, but her feet remained stubbornly in the same spot. So she gave up on her feet, but not the rock. After sitting down to think things over, she strapped the rock to her back with her sash, then got down on her hands and knees and prepared to crawl.

The sun returned to the sky and sent its diffuse light down on the woman's creeping figure. As she started out on the now deserted road, she saw her hands tremble in the sandy soil, probably because they were nervous and unsure about the important task they had suddenly been given. She shared their anxiety; her hands were more deft than her feet, but they were not used to walking. She did not know how to transform her hands into feet; livestock, cats and dogs walked on their hands, but she could not. She was slower than a snake, slower than a lizard.

Her mind was clear as she crawled along with the rock on her back. Afraid that pebbles on the road would wear out Qiliang's winter robe, she rolled it up onto her back and tucked it under the rock. She then resumed crawling, heading towards the outline of the distant mountain. Cooking smoke came from a nearby village; a few people here and there appeared in the bleak fields, but no one came on to the road. No one, that is, except a frog that hopped out from nowhere. She saw it miraculously land on the road, where it hopped along ahead of her, stopping every few hops to wait for her. She could not tell if it was the same blind frog that had left Peach Village with her, but it should not be on the road. She recalled that the frog had given up trying to find its son and had taken over the pit she had dug. Since she could not see its eyes, there was no way she could tell if it was the blind frog from Blue Cloud Prefecture or some unknown frog from Pingyang Prefecture; yet she was sure it was here to show her the way.

As she crawled along, Binu heard the frog point out the route to her.

"Go that way, there's a puddle here. Come this way, there's a pile of excrement. Hurry."

Obeying the frog's commands, Binu crawled and crawled, while the outline of Great Swallow Mountain wavered in front of her, but the frog continued hopping, leading the way, its dark green patterns standing out on the road like a green flame.

Thirteen-Li Shop

The women of Thirteen-Li Shop were gleaning in the field when, to their amazement, they saw the crawling figure. They could not work out why she was crawling, and with a rock on her back at that. Rushing out onto the road, they gathered round and asked many questions, all at the same time. Unable to speak, Binu simply pointed at the outline of Great Swallow Mountain.

"We know where you're going and that your husband must be building the wall," said the women. "What we want to know is: why are you crawling? If you can't walk, then stop and catch your breath before moving on. When do you think you'll get there crawling like this? And with a rock on your back. You gave us quite a fright; we thought you were a gigantic turtle."

Still flat on the ground, one side of her face the colour of mud, Binu reached out to touch one of the women's feet.

Jumping to the side to avoid the hand, the woman nimbly untied the rock on Binu's back and threw it away. You shouldn't carry a rock just because other people do. What's the use of carrying a rock and offering it up to Great Swallow Mountain? The Mountain Deity doesn't see rocks in the hands of the poor. It sees only the rich and powerful, like everyone else."

Binu could not speak, nor did she have the strength to stop the woman from throwing away her rock. So she backed away, trying to reach the spot where the rock had landed. But the woman, still angry, was about to kick the rock off the road when the other women stopped her.

"You can be angry at the rock, but don't make things hard for her. If she wants to offer the rock to the Mountain Deity, let her. You can stop a spirited horse, but not a woman with her mind set on something, for she is willing to suffer for others."

The women carried Binu, along with the rock, over to a haystack, where they gave her some water and washed her face. They smoothed her hair and combed it into a haystack bun, like theirs. With the mud washed away, Binu's young pretty face was revealed, making the women envious. She turned to gaze at the outline of Great Swallow Mountain, her glassy eyes lighting up instantly. The women noticed how bloody her hands were, since they had left a trail of red specks on the haystack.

"We've never seen a woman as devoted as you," one of them said. "The men from Thirteen-Li Shop have all gone to Great Swallow Mountain, but no one has gone looking for them, even though for us it isn't far. Even if your husband was a deity born to the human world, there's no need for you crawl like that. Why not wait here by the haystack for a ride on a donkey cart?"

Binu crawled right back onto the road. The women had never before encountered such a stubborn woman, one who would rather crawl than wait. A woman ran after her with a pair of straw sandals for Binu's hands, but stopped after a few steps, recalling the rumours about female ghosts haunting the road. Villagers claimed to have seen the ghosts late at night, carrying bundles on their head as they trekked north under the moonlight. They disappeared at the sound of humans.

Clasping her chest, the woman cried, "She must be one of the ghosts. They're travelling in broad daylight now!"

She had articulated the suspicion shared by all the others, and that created fervent and fearful responses. "I've always wondered how a living person could feel no pain, so she definitely might be a ghost," one woman said loudly. "No human could tolerate that kind of suffering. Has anyone ever seen a woman carry a rock on her back to search for her husband? Only a ghost could be so determined." They recalled Binu's calm, peaceful look, as well as her cold body.

"What does it matter whether she's a ghost or a human?" said another. "She has a tragic fate as a ghost, and an even more tragic fate if she's human."

Their discussion ended abruptly with startled cries, as an even stranger sight on the road caught their attention. The sand receded wherever the woman crawled, leaving little pools of water on the surface, all linked together; a sparkling stream of water, like a silvery arrow pointing north. With the stream leading the way, a long line of grey-green frogs materialized out of nowhere, forming an impressive army as they hopped towards Great Swallow Mountain. Being northerners, the women had never seen so many frogs. They came from the watery lands of the three southern prefectures; and, carrying the smell of water, they hopped along the trail left by the woman as she crawled towards Great Swallow Mountain. Before the frogs passed, a swarm of white butterflies flew northward above the road. There were plenty of white butterflies in Pingyang Prefecture, but the women had never seen such a dense cloud of them. They flew low, with traces of the warm southern sunlight on their wings, looking like a colourful sash with white piping on its way towards Great Swallow Mountain.

The women cried out again and again in amazement. Looking into the distance, they gazed at the mountain, which they surmised was the destination for the frogs and butterflies. Behind the miraculous sight was a hidden calamity, and suddenly everyone could see the splendid halo of calamity inching towards the mountain. One of the women ran towards the village, shouting, "Prepare the carts; we're going to get our men back. The south has revolted at the death of the King, including even the frogs and butterflies. Who knows what will happen at Great Swallow Mountain."

Great Swallow Mountain

Flying birds did not recognize the Great Wall. A flock of birds migrating south lost their way over Great Swallow Mountain and cried sadly throughout the night. A tiny grey bird crashed into the tent of General Jianyang, commander of the wall-building, at Seven-Yard Terrace. It was a messenger, declaring that a storm of homesickness would soon envelop Great Swallow Mountain.

Every night, General Jianyang went to bed wearing the golden Nine Dragon helmet presented to him by the King. In the morning, the helmet filled up with calls for the workers to build the wall, waking up the General on time. But not this morning, for what echoed inside the helmet was, instead, the sounds of wind, sheep and oxen, as well as a grassland melody he hadn't heard in a long time. It sounded like someone crying and moaning. When he woke up, General Jianyang realized he'd been crying in his sleep; then he saw the little bird, dead by his pillow.

General Jianyang ordered his puzzled steward to fetch a basin of cold water from the mountain spring to save the bird. The constable went for the water, as ordered, but moved slowly, wondering why the General, a cold-hearted man, would care about a little bird. Sensing his puzzlement, the General asked if the constable recalled that the General had come from the steppe in the north, if he recalled that he had once said that an honoured guest on horseback would present him with a congratulatory stole on the day the Great Wall was finished.

"But, General," the constable stammered, "the Wall isn't finished yet, and no one has ridden here."

The General glared at him angrily. "Shangguan Qing, how many times have I told you? Can you remember nothing? The bird will be the bearer of good news when someone comes from the steppe. This grey-beaked bird carries the smell of the steppe and the smell of my family yurt. Come and smell the grease on the bird if you don't believe me."

At Seven-Yard Terrace, General Jianyang personally laid the dead bird in a copper basin, which the constable was about to place on the wall when the General stopped him and ordered him to hold the basin up so that the morning sun could shine on the spring water. "If the bird has come from the steppe," he said, "it will revive when the sun warms up the cold water." He stood on the terrace gazing at the undulating mountains beyond the wall, a rare look of frailness on his ageing face. He said, "The Great Wall should be finished soon; this bird will revive on the day of completion and take me back to the steppe. I must return home to see my parents, my wife and my four children."

The constable held the basin up in the wind, wishing he could tell the General that, even if the bird came back to life, a hundred li of desert still separated the Great Swallow Wall from the wall at Crescent Pass; the two sections of the wall would not be joined in the foreseeable future. The General's thoughts of returning home were like reaching for the moon in the water. He wanted to say, "General, you will die of old age here at Great Swallow Mountain," but he dared not utter those words. In recent days the General's homesickness had made him temperamental and unpredictable. He fantasized daily about finishing the construction overnight, so that he could climb on his horse and return home. When he opened his eyes each morning, the first words he uttered were, "Will the work be done today?" At first, the constable had tried to explain that finishing the wall would take more than a day's work, but his efforts only incurred the General's wrath, which led to slaps across his face. Eventually, he learned his lesson, and, each time the General asked the question, he answered, "Soon, it will soon be done."

Rubbing the Nine Dragon helmet, General Jianyang gazed down at the construction site below the terrace and asked the guard. "Will the work be finished today?"

Avoiding his superior's ardent gaze, the constable looked at the little bird in the water and replied, "Soon. If not today, then tomorrow. General, the wall will be finished soon."

As the bird waited for its rebirth in the water, a morning of accidental sorrow arrived. The sun rose, and along with it, as General Jianyang discovered, the

224

bitter sadness of Great Swallow Mountain erupted. Calls to work that had been loud and clear were stilled on this morning. Porters' baskets moaned forlornly on mountain paths, bricklayers' trowels and stonemasons' chisels sounded dull, causing General Jianying considerable anxiety, for he could not sense the elation of imminent completion. Walking out onto the observation terrace, he saw the construction crew surging all over the mountain. Fire burned bright in the brick kilns; workers carrying dirt and rocks were scattered along the mountain ridge; stonemasons applied their hammers and awls to distant stones. For the first time, the General detected fatigue and sadness on their bodies. Removing his golden helmet, he listened carefully, and thought he heard some indistinct sobbing carried by the wind. He turned to look at the brick kilns, where the sobbing floated in the fire. He turned towards the stone ground, and the sobbing was now echoing in the rocks. He grew even more restless.

"Why didn't I hear the bugle today?" he asked Shangguan Qing. "Instead I hear crying, non-stop crying."

"General, the wind is so strong today that it diffused the sound of the bugle," replied the constable. "The sobbing you hear is probably the wind. The workers at Great Swallow Mountain would not dare cry, so it must be the wind."

Pulling Shangguan Qing over to the side of the city wall, the General insisted that someone was sobbing in the wind. Shangguan said that all he could hear was the wind, not sobs. So the General ordered him to stand on

225

top of the wall and listen carefully. Not daring to disobey, he was helped to the top of the wall, but again he shook his head and said, "General, it is the gusting wind. You have mistaken the sound of flying sand for someone crying."

The General beat him off the wall with his helmet. "How dare you challenge me with those pig's ears of yours!" He went on angrily, "Even the King remembered that I, General Jianyang, come from the steppe. I can hear the steps of wolves from ten li and horses from fifty li. I can hear a storm from a hundred li. But you, all you stupid good-for-nothings, forget that I can even hear my enemy when he pulls his bow outside my tent. So when I say that someone is sobbing on Great Swallow Mountain, then someone must be sobbing. But who is it? I want you to find them."

Shangguan Qing had not expected to be given such a difficult task. Used to catching and arresting people, on this unlucky morning, he was ordered to pursue an imaginary sound. Despite his misgivings, and amid a sea of people on Great Swallow Mountain, Shangguan Qing carried out the order by leading a group of constables to track down the sound.

"Who has been crying?"

"Who cried? Who among you cried? Whoever cried step forward."

Most of the workers stared at Shangguan Qing blankly, posing their own discourses with their eyes. "Who cried? Take a look at our faces, and you'll see there is sweat but no tears. Only someone who has lost his mind would cry; the penalty is forty-seven lashes

226

and carrying forty-seven extra loads of stone. You would need to have a death wish to cry. Besides, why should we? We were born poor, and moving rocks to build a wall is our fate. When our bones are so tired they seem about to fall apart, a good night's sleep will bring them back together, and we go back to work. What's there to cry about?"

Dying men at the hospital faced the search with the same calm and ease. They responded to Shangguan Qing with violent coughs and traces of blood at the corners of their mouths. "I have phlegm, blood and a fever, but no tears. What's the use of shedding tears? There are only so many ways to die, here at Great Swallow Mountain: the escapees are captured and hanged in public; the frail ones, defeated by the rocks and bricks, cough up blood and die; the unlucky ones are infected with plague and die of a high fever; and the stubborn and pessimistic ones jump off a cliff. There you have it; that's how people die around here. When you're not afraid of dying, there's nothing to be afraid of, and when you don't know to be afraid, where should the tears come from?"

Under Shangguan Qing's interrogation, a few workers admitted that they had a sad look, but vehemently denied that they had cried. One young porter from distant Canglan Prefecture said he had felt like crying, but had devised a way to stop the tears from flowing. He stuck out his tongue to show Shangguan Qing and revealed that he bit his tongue whenever he felt like crying. Once the tongue started bleeding, the pain stopped the tears from flowing. Shangguan Qing examined the porter's tongue and discovered that it was indeed a bloody mess, covered with bite marks. The constables were beginning to feel dismayed over their failure to locate the sobbing sound, and some of them whispered about General Jianyang's mental state, which angered Shangguan Qing.

"Underlings are not permitted to criticize their superiors," he said. "If the General said he heard someone crying, then someone must be crying. With the Nine Dragon helmet on his head, the General is smarter than us. If he orders us to locate the wind, we must do it. That goes double for weeping."

When they reached the stone ground, a foreman reported that a woman looking for her husband had cried there that morning. Seeing that she was crawling with a rock on her back, the driver of an oxcart transporting rocks from the quarry had given her a ride out of pity.

Annoyed by the foreman's stammering, Shangguan said angrily, "You're not a child, why can't you give us a decent report? What happened to the woman after she got onto the cart?"

"I can't say. The quarry people are responsible for that," said the foreman, making sure he could not be blamed before continuing. "She was a strange woman. She boarded the cart with the rock on her back, and a frog jumped up with her, upsetting the carter, who said she could bring the rock but not the frog. The woman pleaded on the frog's behalf, saying that one of them was looking for her husband and the other for her son. The frog was here to search for her son!"

"A frog looking for her son?" shouted Shangguan Qing. "Let's get this straight. Where did the frog go? And who is its son?"

"It was a tiny frog, and I don't know where it went. My eyes were on the stonemasons, not the frog. How would I know who the frog's son is?" Seeing the furious look on Shangguan's face, the foreman quickly added, "The woman is here to see Wan Qiliang. She's his wife. That's why she's crawling with that rock on her back and crying."

"You must be the frog's son. Otherwise, how could you be so stupid," said Shangguan. He cast his eyes over the nearby straw sheds and rocks. "Where is the woman? And where is she from?"

"From Blue Cloud Prefecture; she's Wan Qiliang's wife. She said she walked a thousand li, through the whole autumn, to get to Great Swallow Mountain."

"So where is Wan Qiliang? Get him over here."

"We can't. He's dead," said the foreman. "He died in the summer in the rockslide at Broken-Heart Cliff. Sixteen people from Blue Cloud Prefecture died, and Wan Qiliang was one of them, buried alive."

The foreman took a bamboo strip out of a pouch on his back and showed Shangguan Qing the carving, "Blue Cloud Prefecture, Wan Qiliang, Stoneyard, two dry dishes and two liquid dishes." The name was crossed out in red, which made the constable frown.

"He's dead, so why is she here? Take her over to the potter's field and dig up a bone for her. Then send her away with seven sabre coins."

Putting the strip away, the foreman said uncertainly, "We followed the rules and sent her away with a tally to get her sabre coins. But she didn't want the tally, she wanted her husband. Where was I supposed to find him for her? We can't even find his bones. Wan Qiliang's bones aren't buried at the potter's field. He died at Broken-Heart Cliff and, unless we tear down the wall, I can't dig up a bone for her. She was crying at the stoneyard, but I couldn't let her do that. If the General heard her, I'd have been in big trouble. So I told her to cry somewhere else."

"Thinking only about yourself again, I see! Somewhere else is still part of Great Swallow Mountain, and no one is allowed to cry here," yelled the enraged Shangguan Qing.

While leading the constables in a search for the woman from Blue Cloud Prefecture, he detected a gloomy tone in the sounds of the stonemasons chiselling the stones. He noticed that what flew out from under their awls were not rock chips, but sparkling tears, some of which splashed Shangguan in the face; they were boiling hot. He went up to see, first examining the mason's tools, then their eyes and faces.

Pointing at the wet stones, one of the masons said, "Look at the stones. They accumulated so much water overnight we can't wipe them dry."

The stones did look as if they had been dredged out of water, sparkling with moisture. Staring at one of the rocks, Shangguan said, "There was neither rain nor fog last night, so where did the water come from?"

"We don't know," one of the masons said, "but the stones began to weep after Wan Qiliang's wife arrived. We aren't crying, the stones are."

After bringing all those strange tears to the stoneyard, the woman from Blue Cloud Prefecture had disappeared from sight. No one saw where she had gone, as Shangguan Qing discovered after questioning the stonemasons. He suspected them of hiding the truth, but they shook their heads resolutely and said, "We were chiselling stones and have no idea where she went."

A few of them, bolder than the others, had the cheek to be provocative. "A frog was showing the woman the way and, since we are not frogs, how could we know where she went?"

In the end, it was an honest, elderly worker who cleared up the constables' confusion. Pointing to the rocks on the ground, he said, "Follow the watery rocks if you want to find her. They are wet wherever she has crawled."

The Great Wall

A silhouette of rolling hills was carved out of the northern sky; between the sky and the hills was the long, curving Great Swallow Mountain Wall. Under the early winter sun, it gave off a razor-sharp white light, lending the sky a tired, despondent look. The Great Wall was in reality a long, unending fence that scaled mountains and climbed hills, stretching into the distance along the mountainous contour. It looked like a white coiled dragon, but was actually a fence that straddled mountains, a great many of them, wearing a row of stiff caps and sashes on the peaks, and one of those capped and sashed sections was the Great Swallow Mountain.

The workers on Great Swallow Mountain saw Wan Qiliang's wife, who, like a tiny piece of black jewellery, was now studded on the top of Broken-Heart Cliff.

Cradling a rock in her arms, she knelt on the cliff and cried. No one could understand how a sickly woman carrying a rock could negotiate those steep hills and narrow rugged paths. Someone said it was a magic frog that had led her there, but not everyone believed him.

Seeing the vultures circling above the woman, someone else said, "Broken-Heart Cliff is so steep and so high, even a frog can't get up there. It must have been a vulture that took her up."

Floating clouds drifted over the cliff. Men who were building the wall at mid-slope sometimes saw the tiny figure of Binu when the clouds disappeared. They heard the howling of the wind but not her cries, though every gust from Broken-Heart Cliff sounded like sobbing and, like the wind from the south, left a moist, sticky pall on the workers. The porters carrying rocks to higher places gathered on the cliff like clouds, but quickly dispersed. When they heard at mid-slope that a woman from Blue Cloud Prefecture had dragged a strange trail of water with her, the porters from her home prefecture easily located her by following the water marks. But they shook their heads in disappointment and left when they saw her tearful face.

"It's not my wife," each of them said. "I knew my own wife could not endure that much hardship."

Some people, having heard at the foothills that Wan Qiliang's wife was on the cliff, followed the water trail, still carrying rocks in their baskets, as if running after their own wives. They stopped below Broken-Heart Cliff.

"What a pitiable woman that wife of Wan Qiliang is. She walked a thousand li to deliver winter clothes, but there's no one to wear them now. Wan Qiliang left nothing behind, not even a bone. Look at that winter robe, rolled up on her back. Now there's no one to wear it."

233

All the porters walked past her like floating clouds, except for one called Xiaoman, who had been given an unusual task. Carrying a pair of empty baskets on his pole, he followed the trail up to Broken-Heart Cliff and stopped when he saw Binu. After filling one of the baskets with rocks, he kicked the other one over to Binu.

"You must be Wan Qiliang's wife. Get into that basket. Shangguan Qing cannot make it up this high, so he told me to put rocks in one basket and you in the other and take you down the mountain."

Binu looked at the basket, then slowly removed the robe with green piping and put it in the basket.

"Not the robe!" said Xiaoman. "He wants *you* in the basket."

Picking up her rock again, Binu said to Xiaoman, "Retribution. This is retribution. Heaven would not permit Qiliang to wear a robe that I had taken by force in Five-Grain City."

Xiaoman had no idea what she was talking about, so he picked up the robe and shook it. "It's a nice, warm winter robe. Why throw *it* away instead of that rock? You have no use for the rock now that he's dead. You cannot change things, no matter how many rocks you offer to the Mountain Deity. Now, hurry up, put on the robe and climb into my basket. I'll take you down to get Wan Qiliang's tally. That way you'll receive seven sabre coins."

Binu kicked the robe away and said again, "Retribution. This is retribution. How could Qiliang possibly wear a robe that was taken by force?"

234

"Don't speak to the valleys below. I'm talking to you." Xiaoman angrily walked over to the cliff's edge, where he saw a blue mountain mist spreading across the valley. "There's nothing but the blue mist left. Ever since the accident at Broken-Heart Cliff, the valley has been shrouded in mist, day and night. They say it's the spirits of the dead. What's the point of talking to the mist? You can't take a spirit back with you, anyway."

Binu pointed down at the valley and opened her mouth, as if to speak, but Xiaoman heard nothing. He saw, instead, her tear-stricken face and drops of sparkling water raining down from her fingers.

"Why all those tears?" Startled by Binu's mournful face, Xiaoman instinctively covered his eyes and shouted, "I'm from Fort Double Dragon at the base of North Mountain. Only a single mountain separates our two villages. I know that people from that region are not allowed to shed tears. When your husband dies, you must cry with your ears, your lips or your hair. How can you shed tears with your eyes? You mustn't cry with your eyes!"

But the tears gushed from her eyes, like spring water spewing across mountains and forests. She appeared to have forgotten the Peach Village *Rulebook for Daughters*. She cried with abandon and pointed at the valley, while saying something to Xiaoman. But he heard only ear-piercing shrieks.

"A grave, you say? You want a grave?" He tried with difficulty to decipher the words by reading her lips. "Where am I supposed to find a grave in the valley? This is the Great Wall, not Peach Village. You can't dig a grave wherever you like. There is a potter's field on the western slope, and that is where all those who died at Great Swallow Mountain are buried. Quick, get into the basket and let me take you there. You can dig a grave for Wan Qiliang."

Binu's cracked lips were also brimming with tears, as her cries turned to wails. Her voice was unworldly. Xiaoman suddenly heard something clearly.

"Bones," she murmured. "Bones, where are the bones?"

"What bones are you talking about? You think you are going to retrieve his bones? You won't find them. Over a dozen men died in the landslide at Broken-Heart Cliff, and they are all buried under the rubble. With the wall built on top of them, they have become part of its foundation." Beginning to lose patience, Xiaoman pulled out a ball of hemp and said, "No more crying. Do you know what this is? Shangguan Qing told me to gag you with it. There's a rule here that, no matter how sad you may be, you cannot cry, not at North Mountain, and not here. General Jianyang hates the sound of weeping, he says it disturbs the workers and delays the work." Xiaoman tipped the basket over and pointed to its opening. "Get in, or I'll be in big trouble. Big Sister, please don't get me into trouble. You are the wife of Wan Qiliang, and we are from the same area. I'd rather not handle you as if I were moving rocks, so please get in there of your own accord."

Binu pushed the basket aside and turned away. Xiaoman picked it up and stood in front of her, obviously ready to put his pole to use if necessary. "We are all unfortunate people," he said angrily. "You are not the only woman whose husband died, and you are not the only one who wants to cry. My three brothers and I came here together, and now I am the only one left. You can cry all you want, but do you know how many people will suffer because of it? I'm going to count to three, and then I'll pick you up if you won't get in the basket on your own."

Pointing his pole at Binu, he began to count. Binu stopped crying at the count of one, and struggled to her feet at the count of two. When he counted three, Xiaoman realized that she was preparing to jump off the cliff. Dropping his pole, he rushed over, grabbed her and carried her back to the basket. She was light as a feather, but abundant water from her body splashed him in the face. He was rubbing his eyes, which had been forced shut by the tears, when he heard a crackling noise coming from his basket. It was the sound of the willow rotting away from the assault of tears.

"Don't cry. Your tears are ruining my basket. Without it, we can't get down, and you'll have to jump. Then what will I do? I'll have to jump with you." He could not keep his eyes dry, but quickly discovered that the tears were his own. He strained to keep his eyes open, while looping the pole through the basket handles; they snapped off the instant he tried to lift the pole. "Didn't I tell you not to cry? See, you've ruined the handles of my basket. Now how can I take you down?" He raised his pole, but it fell to the ground. Then he saw a familiar face, ancient like that of his mother and sad like that of his sister. The woman sat in the basket, like his mother or his sister, crying to him. A watery sky spread out in her eyes and rain began to fall. Xiaoman sat down on his pole and sobbed.

From the valley beneath Broken-Heart Cliff the souls of the dead arose and spread through the air like a fog. The valley was bathed in a tearful white light; the wind and clouds sobbed in mid-air; trees and grass cried on the hills; tears flowed from rocks, from dark green bricks, and from yellow earth on the wall. A hawk skimmed past Xiaoman's head, sending drops of cold water down on his forehead; he assumed they were hawk's tears. He heard the baskets crying to each other; it was impossible to tell which basket cried louder, which was sadder. The sun shimmered. Xiaoman was about to search for the sun's tears when he heard a northern wind rise up and send a gust of yellow sand rolling across the mountains and over the ridges. Through the flying sand, he saw Wan Qiliang's wife crawl out of the basket and untie the gourd at her waist. He saw her final arrangements for the gourd, and how it tumbled over the wall and rolled down the steep hill. He could not tell whether she had offered the gourd to the valley or to Qiliang's soul. For the first time in his life, he heard a gourd crack open and saw an eruption of bright shiny tears gush from it, like bolts of lightning. He saw the tears plunge into the valley; Great Swallow Mountain trembled and the Great Wall shook imperceptibly. An indescribable terror overcame Xiaoman, for he sensed that the mountain was on the verge of splitting open. He cried out to Binu, who was standing at the edge of the cliff, "The mountain is crumbling. Don't stand there. Come back to the basket."

Binu knelt in the sand and wind, and banged against the wall. Finally she was able to cry out, "Qiliang, Qiliang, come out." She pounded and pounded. "Qiliang, Qiliang, come out or let me in."

The wall, the store of arrows and the beacon tower all resounded to the pounding of the grieving woman. The rocks and the dirt let out muffled rumbles. Wind was now coming from every direction, hitting Xiaoman in the face with yellow sand that was sharper than knives. Terrified, he picked up a basket and ran down the slope, but threw it away when he saw that it was now filled with frogs from the ponds and rice fields of Blue Cloud Prefecture that were croaking in a hoarse but unified voice. He shouted at Binu, "Big Sister, please don't cry. You cannot cry. The frogs are here to cry in your place." He snatched the pole and kept running down the hill. Flowing yellow sand was creating steps down the hill, up which a swarm of beetles was climbing. He knew they were insects that could cry. In the spring, they ate leaves in Blue Cloud Prefecture's mulberry groves. Each bite of a leaf brought forth a teardrop of remorse. Xiaoman made way for the beetles and turned to shout, "Big Sister, don't cry. You'll run out of tears. You cannot cry. The beetles are here to cry in your place."

He kept running down the hill, encountering white butterflies with beautiful golden marks etched on the tips of their wings. He knew they were golden thread butterflies, native to North Mountain, where they were rumoured to be the three hundred spirits that had cried for their wronged ancestors. When he looked up to watch the butterflies flying past him, drops of warm butterfly tears fell on his face. He wiped his face, and held up his pole to welcome the spirits of his ancestors. But the butterflies did not land on his pole, and he knew that they no longer recognized him. The spirits of his wronged ancestors had forgotten a descendant who had been away for so many years. They had flown over a thousand li to come to Great Swallow Mountain, to cry with Qiliang's wife at Broken-Heart Cliff.

Xiaoman ran down the hill until he reached a beacon tower, where he met Shangguan Qing and his dejected constables. Carrying ropes in their hands, they headed for higher ground to look in the direction of Broken-Heart Cliff.

"Where's the woman we told you to carry down?" they demanded of Xiaoman. "Why is she crying on Broken-Heart Cliff and making the mountain quake?"

Ignoring their outstretched hands and their ropes, he kept running. He saw a group of workers near a pile of arrows; they had put their work aside and were engaged in a heated discussion. They waved when they saw him. "Stop running. There is no more work. Even General Jianyang has stopped working. He has mounted his horse and is following a bird back to the steppe."

"You can't work even if you want to." Xiaoman shouted back at them. "Wan Qiliang's wife's tears have

240

brought down the Great Wall." He turned and pointed at the cliff. "Can you hear that? Listen! It is the sound of the mountain crumbling. The wall at Broken-Heart Cliff has collapsed. Wan Qiliang and the others are rising up from the ground!"

Where Three Roads Meet

Salley Vickers

At the end of his life, an old man waits in his office for a stranger to arrive. Over the next few weeks, Teiresias will visit again, making his way across the heath to relate the story of his life. As these two men sit together, a remarkable tale unfolds.

The compelling story of Oedipus, who, unknowingly, kills his father and marries his mother, is probably the most influential of all the Greek myths, having furnished Freud's theory of psychoanalysis. Bestselling novelist Salley Vickers, herself a former psychoanalyst, takes the ancient story of patricide and incest and explores it through the vision of Teiresias, the blind seer, who alone "sees" the truth about the protagonists' terrible past and their place in the cosmic order.

ISBN 978-0-7531-8064-8 (hb)
ISBN 978-0-7531-8065-5 (pb)

Girl Meets Boy

Ali Smith

Girl meets boy. It's a story as old as time. But what happens when an old story meets a brand new set of circumstances?

Ali Smith's re-mix of Ovid's most joyful metamorphosis is a story about the kind of fluidity that can't be bottled and sold.

It is about girls and boys, girls and girls, love and transformation, a story of puns and doubles, reversals and revelations.

Funny and fresh, poetic and political, Girl Meets Boy is a myth of metamorphosis for the modern world.

(from website)

ISBN 978-0-7531-8060-0 **(hb)**
ISBN 978-0-7531-8061-7 **(pb)**

Dream Angus

Alexander McCall Smith

If he's in the right mood, divine Angus might grant you sight of your true love in a dream; you might even fall in love with him — but he'll never love you back. He's too busy making mischief — stealing the palace of the gods from his father, turning his enemies into pigs etc — until he is trapped by his own romantic games and falls for an unattainable woman, doomed to seek her forever.

In 20th century Scotland, Angus's troubled alter ego searches for his true family; a psychotherapist who helps people understand their dreams, his life seems to parallel that of his mythic namesake, until we ask — could they be the one and the same?

Mesmerically weaving together the tales of the Celtic god and the Scottish scientist, Alexander McCall Smith unites dream and reality, leaving us to wonder: what is life, but the pursuit of our dreams?

ISBN 978-0-7531-7718-1 (hb)
ISBN 978-0-7531-7719-8 (pb)

Lion's Honey

David Grossman

Samson the hero; a brave warrior, leader of men and Nazarite of God? Or a misfit given to whoring and lust, who failed to fulfil his destiny? In Lion's Honey, award-winning writer David Grossman takes on one of the most vivid and controversial characters in the Bible. Revisiting Samson's famous battle with the lion, his many women and his betrayal by them all — including the only one he ever loved — Grossman gives us a provocative new take on the story and its climax, Samson's final act of death, bringing down a temple on himself and 3,000 Philistines. In exhilarating and lucid prose, Grossman reveals the journey of a single, lonely, tortured soul who never found a true home in the world, who was uncomfortable in his very body and who, some might say, was the precursor of today's suicide bombers.

ISBN 978-0-7531-7716-7 **(hb)**
ISBN 978-0-7531-7717-4 **(pb)**